LESSONS IN LOVE
Book One:
A Cambridge Fellows Mystery

CHARLIE COCHRANE

LESSONS IN LOVE
Book One: A Cambridgxe Fellows Mystery
Copyright © Charlie Cochrane, 2008
Cover art by Dan Skinner and Beverly Maxwell
ISBN Trade paperback: 978-1-60202-148-8
ISBN MS Reader (LIT): 978-1-60202-149-5
Other available formats (no ISBNs are assigned):
PDF, PRC & HTML

Linden Bay Romance, LLC
Palm Harbor, Florida 34684
www.lindenbayromance.com

This is a work of fiction and any resemblance to persons, living or dead, or business establishments, events or locales is coincidental.

All Rights Are Reserved. No part of this may be used or reproduced in any manner whatsoever without written permission, except in the case of brief quotations embodied in critical articles and reviews.

First Linden Bay Romance publication: November 2008

This book would never have happened had it not been for a wonderful group of friends. They know who they are and they have my heartfelt thanks.

And for my much-loved family—who'd have thought the old gal had it in her?

Chapter One

"That is my chair, sir." The voice was deep, sharp, and shattered Dr. Stewart's concentration.

He looked up to see a stern looking young man towering over him. *Well, not necessarily that young*, Stewart reflected, *he must be nearly my age, but he has such a lean, youthful look about him, you might think he's just an undergraduate.* He swiftly took in a pair of chocolate brown eyes—eyes that lurked below black, curly hair, which seemed to want to cover them—a handsome face, and a very bony frame. He rose immediately.

"I do apologize, sir. I've only arrived at St. Bride's today and I haven't been appraised of all the customs and habits. I hope that you'll forgive me." Stewart produced what he hoped was a winning smile and bowed politely.

The other man harrumphed and nodded slightly in return. "There are a number of traditions we cling to here, Mr...."

"Stewart, Dr. Stewart. The college authorities saw fit enough to forget the indiscretions of my undergraduate years here and have appointed me to a fellowship in English." He grinned again, emphasizing the contrast to the man who spoke to him. Stewart seemed to be born to wear a smile, while the other appeared as if he'd never smiled in his life.

"Well, Stewart, we are great ones for resisting change, and the particular chair a man inhabits after high table is regarded as sacrosanct." The severe looking man pointed to the empty seat next to him. "This place never seems to be occupied; perhaps you might like to use it?"

Stewart could guess why that chair was never used but decided he'd take the risk. "How long have you been at St. Bride's? I can't place you from my earlier time here." He would have remembered if he'd met him before, of course. He'd noticed this man at high table, not just for his striking good looks but for his apparent unease with joining in the conversation around him—except for one occasion when he seemed to be extremely animated and the words 'differential calculus' had been mentioned. *Bet he's a mathematician. They're all as mad as hatters.*

"I've been here six years, Dr. Stewart, ever since I took my degree. I have the honor to be working under Professor Moore teaching mathematics." For the first time the stranger looked fully into his companion's face. "I suppose you'll be with Professor Goodridge?"

"Oh, no, not clever enough by half to be with the fellows who delve into Anglo-Saxon. The Bard of Avon is my concern," Stewart saw the puzzled expression on the other man's face and grinned. "Shakespeare, I mean. As a man of logic and higher reasoning you'll please forgive the whimsy of a mere playgoer."

The other man looked closely at Stewart again, obviously suspicious that he was being made game of, then seemed to decide that the remarks were kindly meant and almost smiled. "Even a pupil of Euclid can recognize the value of Shakespeare's works. Indeed, I was named after one of his characters."

Dr. Stewart couldn't have been more stunned; the man's hard-faced exterior didn't suggest a romantic name.

Lessons in Love

"Hamlet, Jacques—which is it?"

"Orlando. I was christened Orlando."

Stewart waited to see if a surname would follow, decided that it wouldn't, so spoke himself. "You're very lucky. My parents saw fit to name me Jonathan—the only thing in my life that I've not forgiven them for. I'm Jonty to all those who want to use the name."

The mention of parents had caused a small cloud to pass over Orlando's face and he began staring at his feet. Stewart pressed on, unable to stop gabbling in the face of such studied non-communication. "Are there any other customs I must seek not to break?"

The question never got answered, as the Jove-like figure of Dr. Peters, the Master of St. Bride's, approached. "I beg you not to get up, gentlemen. I was coming to introduce you to each other, our numerical genius not having been here before dinner when Dr. Stewart met the rest of the fellows—but I see that you've already made Dr. Coppersmith's acquaintance."

Coppersmith—no wonder he was so unwilling to tell me. His parents certainly gave him an unlucky combination of names; perhaps that's why he always looks so cross. "Dr. Coppersmith has been instructing me in the college ways, in case I make some dreadful error of etiquette."

Jonty inclined his head to express his gratitude—his mathematical colleague looked sterner than ever. "I'm honored to be able to share some of our little ways with Dr. Stewart and hope that he'll profit from being back at our college. I wish you good night, gentlemen—I have a lecture to deliver in the morning and must take my rest." Coppersmith rose, bowed his head and departed, leaving the other two men rather speechless.

Later, as Jonty walked slowly back to his rooms, he chuckled quietly. *I'd give a five pound note to be at that mathematics lecture tomorrow and I bet most of the students would give five pounds to miss it.* But for all that his new colleague seemed—on the surface at least—to be a pompous prig, his face stayed in Stewart's mind until he fell asleep.

St. Bride's wasn't one of the most notable Cambridge colleges, lacking the grandeur of St. John's or Trinity. It formed a little backwater where life had changed very little over the last four hundred years, but small adjustments were made from time to time. The chair next to Orlando's very soon became associated with Stewart. They sat together almost every evening after high table, chatting over coffee or port. The dons who'd known Coppersmith since his arrival at the college were astounded. He was notorious for being a solitary fellow, never one to indulge in college chat or even in most of the discussion in the Senior Common Room. Unless it was about maths, of course, when he would contribute freely and with amazing perception, before clamming up if the subject strayed a little. And yet there he was, evening after evening, talking away to Dr. Stewart, and sometimes even smiling. What they talked about, none of the other dons would've hazarded a guess, nor why they had struck up such an unlikely alliance.

If they'd have asked Stewart, he'd have told them he'd come back to his old college hoping to make a fresh start and acquire new friends in the process. He'd have wondered with them about the fact that he and Coppersmith had hit it off immediately, after their first meeting, both gradually realizing the few things they had in common were more interesting than the things in which they differed. He wouldn't have told them that he found Orlando enormously attractive and that being with the man was a constant pleasure.

In Jonty's thoughts alone he would compare their meeting to that of Rosalind and *her* Orlando, an instant magnetism drawing him to the other man. He wasn't stupid enough to confess that. Even if the traditions of this college, within this University, made it possible to remain an old bachelor, surrounded by other old bachelors, and have no one raise an eyebrow, there were still dangers. Public disgrace, prosecution. He would risk them both if he formed, again, an alliance with another man within the walls of St. Bride's. For the moment he would have to savor the budding friendship with this strange young chap and hope against hope that the attraction might prove to be mutual.

Anyone asking Coppersmith the same question, about why he'd suddenly found himself an acquaintance, wouldn't have received any sort of an answer. Not just because he kept his feelings to himself, but because he couldn't say at this point why he felt so differently about Jonty than he felt about all the other dons. Why he should want to spend time with the man, when he'd been solitary all his life. The University part of his mind might have said that it was the classic case of opposites attracting, the properties of poles of magnets or particles of different charge. The personal part wouldn't have commented as it had no idea what was going on.

"You didn't take your degree here, Coppersmith. Which seat of learning did you grace with your incredible skills?"

"I was at Oxford, Stewart—Gabriel College." Orlando settled into his seat, more comfortable then he'd been at any point since he came to Cambridge. More comfortable than he'd been since he was a child. For the first time in his life, it seemed like he'd made a friend and the experience was all a bit startling.

"If I had known the University would stoop so low as to take someone from *the other place* I would never have agreed to return." Jonty grinned; he seemed to spend half his life grinning, or smiling, or smirking, and that unsettled Orlando, too, although he couldn't work out why just yet.

Coppersmith wondered whether there was some fixed amount of cheerfulness allowed in the universe and if his companion's excess compensated for his own apparent lack of it. He'd become quietly accustomed to the happy presence in the adjacent chair, even though such a thing would have horrified him only a few weeks ago. He'd never wanted to share his thoughts—unless they were to do with numbers—with anyone else and now he was gossiping away like one of the college cleaning ladies.

He cast a furtive glance at his companion, who was struggling with a pair of nutcrackers and a wayward walnut. Jonty's unruly blond hair was all over the place, his blue eyes showed unusual depths of concentration and his tongue was poking out slightly, as it often did when he tackled a difficult task. Coppersmith had never before appreciated that Stewart possessed a handsome face and the realization was a great shock to him. He could define the most obscure bits of calculus, look at a problem and solve it almost instantly, but he'd never really understood what people meant when they mentioned beauty. Not until now, when it was sitting right next to him.

"Got the little bugger in the end!" Jonty beamed triumphantly, offering his friend half of his newly released treasure. No one had ever used the word *bugger* in the Senior Common Room before, was never likely to again, but somehow the more colorful aspects of Stewart's speech were tolerated in a way that would be unlikely with anyone else.

They often talked about sport—discovering that they'd each won a rugby blue but hadn't managed to play against the other, being picked in different years. Coppersmith had been a wing three-quarter, naturally, given his wiry physique—lacking in grace but fast. He'd scored twice in the Varsity match, despite finishing on the losing side.

"I suppose you were in the front row?" Orlando drew his conclusions from Jonty's muscular frame.

"Coppersmith! Do my ears look as if they have spent time in a scrum?"

They didn't; Orlando thought that they were rather

Lessons in Love

shapely ears and that was a shock to him, too. To be sitting in the SCR of his college and musing about how attractive the man sitting next to you seemed was beyond his imaginings. Making a friend had been enough of a surprise; this was staggering.

"I was scrum half, and a very wily one was how *The Times* described me. Shame that we lost that year, like you the next; your selectors seemed to have imported an entire troop of gorillas to play in your pack. One of them broke my finger." Jonty held up the joint in question and smirked. "I broke his nose." He began to laugh, his bright blue eyes crinkling up with the sheer joy of being alive and in the company of someone he liked. Orlando began to laugh, too—for the first time in what seemed ages. When they stopped—out of breath and in disgrace with the rest of the fellows—Coppersmith knew that their friendship had been cemented.

Dr. Coppersmith was supposed to be marking papers from his students, but he was more interested in watching, through his window, the progress of a golden head across the court. *That's my friend Dr. Stewart. He walks along the river with me and listens to all my latest theories, even if he doesn't understand a word of them.* Three weeks previously, Orlando had no one in his life he could ever call friend. Then, into his world of gown-black and stone-grey, half tones and half a life, had come this vision of blue and gold, like a ray of spring sunshine against a cloudless sky.

My friend, Dr. Stewart. We go to chapel together and he's never bothered that I sing all the hymns and responses out of tune. It was strange for Orlando to have reached the age of twenty-eight without finding anybody he wanted to be close to. His life had been bound by the university, the college and mathematics—all of them important and serious. And now he'd found that most frivolous of things—someone to share his thoughts and ideas with—although in reality Jonty had come along and found him, stealing his chair in the process. It made Orlando feel more alive than he'd ever felt and more than a little frightened.

My friend, Dr. Stewart. He comes along and says "We've been invited to drinks, Dr. Coppersmith, so get your best bib and tucker ready!" We. Suddenly Orlando had a social life, whether he wanted one or not, and it was as part of a pairing. Somehow all the things he'd always dreaded—making small talk, being sociable—had become possible, so long as he had his colleague with him to jolly him along. Unexpectedly, life had a distinctly more enjoyable flavor.

Coppersmith turned his attention back to the papers on his desk, only to find that he'd written *My friend, Dr. Stewart* on the topmost one and now had to scratch it out furiously before anyone noticed.

"Will you come and take a cup of coffee or a glass of port in my rooms, Stewart?"

It was evening and the Senior Common Room had been overrun by strangers. There were women visiting, patronesses of the college to be sure, but still female and therefore to be treated with caution by most of the fellows. Especially by Coppersmith, who, though he was now brave enough to talk to almost any woman, even one from Girton, was still extremely unhappy in their company.

Jonty almost choked on his answer. He'd been waiting weeks for an invitation to Orlando's set of room. All he'd managed so far was to poke his little nose around the door before being whisked away—and now it had come like a bolt out of the blue. 1906 had dawned and the new year and the new term seemed to have made Coppersmith bold.

"I think that we'd better. Don't look over there just now, but there are two skirted bottoms occupying *our* chairs." Stewart sniggered.

Orlando looked horrified, as though he'd have to have the things fumigated before they could sit there again.

Lessons in Love

"Come on, then, before we're forced into conversation." A sudden disconcerting thought must have occurred to him. "Unless you want to stay, of course?" One of the ladies was quite young and Coppersmith asked Jonty whether she would be described as pretty. Perhaps, he suggested, Stewart would like to talk to her—he always seemed to have no problem chatting with females and they positively flocked around him.

Jonty took his time before answering. "No, I'd be more than content with a glass of some pleasant brew and a little peace and quiet."

They found a whole bottle of a really good port—most welcome, as both of them had been extremely sober at table due to the unnerving presence of the petticoat brigade. Jonty settled into one of Orlando's worn but comfortable armchairs and enjoyed the glow from the fire. While his friend poured the port, Stewart drank in his surroundings. The room contained the usual Bride's mix of the academic, the sporting and the personal, very little of the last compared to the first. It was what his mother would have described as *being part of a house, dear, not a home*, and it gave away very little about its owner. He found that disappointing, as his family had plied him with questions about the mysterious Dr. Coppersmith all over the Christmas break and he'd not been really able to answer them adequately.

He's my friend, Mama, and I enjoy his company very much, had been as far as it had gone, even under his mother's third degree. Although if he were being honest, Orlando meant a lot more to him than just being a colleague. Jonty's opinion of his friend had gradually changed from *pompous ass* to *treasured companion* and he knew that he was beginning to harbor more than just platonic thoughts about the man. Being in his rooms, now, watching him simply wrestling with a Brazil nut and the crackers was a true pleasure. Orlando's dark hair was highlighted by the fire's glow and a halo of light gave him the appearance of a somewhat serious angel. Jonty could feel his heart beating faster as he savored the sight.

"Much nicer here than in with those women, eh, Dr. Stewart?"

"It is indeed, Dr. Coppersmith. Deal us a hand of whist and we'll make an evening of it." Jonty watched Orlando poke around in a draw for a deck, admiring the fact that even his rummaging was a neat and ordered process. Coppersmith truly was both the strangest and loveliest of creatures.

"Why don't you call me Jonty? I think, Dr. Coppersmith, that we're friends enough now to lose some of the formality." Dr. Stewart had just lost his third consecutive game of cards, the clock's hands were nearing half past ten and the evening had been enjoyable for them both.

Dr. Coppersmith considered—it was as if he had to find the second differential of *Jonathan* before he could answer. "I think that I could call you *Jonty* here in my rooms, but I don't think that it would be appropriate anywhere else." Orlando was embarrassed enough about all the occasions he'd doodled *My friend Dr. Stewart* on things; it would be awful if he were caught writing *My friend Jonty.* "I suspect I'm too far set in my ways."

"That would be absolutely fine—if I may call you Orlando, in return?"

It was the strangest thing, but Coppersmith felt decidedly peculiar when his friend said *Orlando*—the first time Stewart had ever used the name, he realized. It was turning out to be an evening of firsts. The first time he'd had another one of the fellows of Bride's in his room other than on college business. The first use of his Christian name. The first time he'd had this peculiar fluttering in his stomach that he couldn't put a cause to. "It would be an honor so to be addressed."

Lessons in Love

Jonty simply smiled in the face of such affectedness, rather than breaking into his usual laughter. Coppersmith knew that he became pompous when he felt some deep emotion and Stewart must have recognized the fact. Perhaps the man found this trait rather touching. Whatever he was thinking, Jonty rose and moved to the mantelpiece, picking up a gilt-framed photograph, the only one in the room that had no obvious university link. "May I, Orlando? Is this your mother and father?" He was watching his friend's face out of the corner of his eye and must have seen the discomfort there.

Orlando nodded. He didn't really want to speak as he was sure his voice would tremble and he had no idea why that should be. It wasn't just at the mention of his parents; every time he looked at Jonty, the fluttering got worse.

"It's extraordinary how much you resemble your mother—do you see very much of them?" Stewart held the picture at arm's length and compared it to the handsome man across the room.

There was a long pause. "They're both dead—my mother didn't survive to see me take my degree." Coppersmith began to study his hands.

Stewart looked full of remorse for the distress he was causing. "I'm so sorry, Orlando, I didn't know. I can't imagine what life would be like without one's parents in the background—it makes me sad to think that yours didn't see the success you have made of yourself."

Coppersmith looked blankly around his room to see if he could see any signs of the success to which Stewart referred; there wasn't any obvious evidence. "I have some more pictures of them," he said finally, "if you'd like to see them."

"But of course I would." Jonty sat down again, watching while Orlando rummaged in another drawer and produced a small photograph album. He brought the album over, sitting on the floor next to Stewart's feet and placing the book on his friend's lap, accidentally brushing his hand against the man's leg in the process.

Just the barest touch—no more than a hairsbreadth of contact, but it had sparked like static between them. Coppersmith froze, his heart racing at the effect on him the touch had made. This feeling was unlike anything he'd ever known before and he still couldn't put a name or meaning to it. He gingerly placed his hand next to Stewart's on the velvet cover of the album; their eyes met and held—dark staring into light—until they could look no more.

"Orlando," Jonty whispered, raising his hand until it was almost touching the other man's face. "I..."

There was a loud and persistent rapping at the door and Coppersmith became aware of three things. Firstly that his heart was pounding so strongly that he wasn't sure any ribcage could contain it. Secondly that Jonty was muttering *Damn it. Damn it and blast it*, over and over. Thirdly that someone might just be trying to gain their attention. He rose and stumbled to the door.

"Dr. Coppersmith, sir." It was Summerbee, out of breath from running up from the porters' lodge. "It's young Lord Morcar. I thought I would come to you, seeing as he is one of your pupils."

"And what is it about Lord Morcar that can't wait until morning?"

"He's dead, sir. His friends found him not five minutes since—we've sent for the doctor, but I thought you should..." He tailed off, seemingly unsure of himself.

"Has the Master been informed?" A frightened look on the porter's face told Coppersmith that the man was hoping he would take that particular burden from him. He would not. "You must do it immediately. I'll go to his Lordship's room—which is it?"

"The Old Court, J7, sir." Summerbee touched his bowler and departed, probably full of dread at the prospect of knocking at the hallowed door of the Master's lodge.

Coppersmith turned and saw Stewart watching him. He wondered whether Jonty would be astounded at the command that he'd shown with the porter, how his shy, socially uncomfortable friend had transformed into a man of authority and action. Orlando felt quite proud of himself, even if he was disappointed at the interruption.

"Jonty, will you come with me?"

Stewart didn't hesitate to show his full agreement. "Of course, if you want me to."

"It's not a matter of wanting. I'm going to need you there, I think." All the flutterings in his stomach had faded now, driven off by the thought of a dead man, but he still wanted Jonty beside him.

As they made their way over to The Old Court, they regretted their lack of prudence in terms of overcoats. The harsh East Anglian wind, *straight from Siberia*, the locals said, carried snow with it, and they felt chilled to the bones. A crowd of undergraduates had gathered at the bottom of the staircase, being kept from the room itself only by the burly form of Lee, another of the porters. Coppersmith tried to make his way through them, but they took no notice of him; they were excited and afraid, and some of them beginning to show signs of hysteria.

This time Jonty took control. Dr. Stewart was popular among the undergraduates, being the most open and approachable of all the fellows at St. Bride's. Although he was merciless in pulling apart any essay he felt was poorly written or ill-researched, he did it with such kindness and good humor that none of them took umbrage, and they all tried harder the next time.

"Gentlemen!" Jonty's tones split the night and brought all the chattering to a halt. "Thank you. It does no one any good you staying out here freezing to..." he was about to say *death* but thought better of it. "Freezing to the ground. I would suggest that unless you have something useful to say about this to either the doctor or the Master, you return to your own rooms." The gathering broke up, aided by the threat of Jove's imminent arrival and the especial efforts of one young man who Stewart suspected had a bit of a crush on his English tutor and who was, no doubt, determined to see his idol obeyed.

Orlando was able to get up the stairs at last and into the room, leaving Stewart with Lee to await the Master. He seemed to be gone an inordinate length of time, making Jonty bold enough to venture up. He found his friend standing rigidly over the half dressed body of a lad of about twenty—a slim, angular young man, pale in life and milk white now. The room was freezing, the window open wide; Stewart reached over to shut it.

"Don't touch anything!" Orlando's voice was as icy as the glittering windowpanes. "Look at this, Dr. Stewart," he pointed to the young lad's throat, ashen but mottled with ugly contusions. "I believe Lord Morcar has been strangled."

Jonty reflected that it had certainly been a night full of revelations and this had been perhaps one surprise too far.

Chapter Two

It was a long night, a series of uncomfortable conversations in that cold set of rooms in the presence of that cold body. Dr. Peters arrived, huffing and blustering at being roused from his bed, anger turning to horror as he became aware that what he'd no doubt expected—heart failure or an awkward fall—was far from the unpleasant reality. A murder, here in *his* college, was unthinkable, or so he'd told Coppersmith and Stewart.

"My only consolation is that it must have been someone from outside St. Bride's who has committed this despicable deed."

Stewart pointed out the fact of the victim's partial undress and this disturbed Dr. Peters, too.

"Perhaps he was changing for bed when he was disturbed…?" The words sounded thin and unconvincing; everyone present was aware that the disheveled state of the corpse suggested that some form of romantic activity had occurred.

"I hate to make the suggestion, Master, but could his Lordship have brought a young lady into St. Bride's?" Dr. Coppersmith was being unusually bold.

"Perhaps, but I fail to see how she could have left without being noticed." There had been a number of inappropriate visitors recently and the college authorities had decided to keep a very close eye on all who came and went after dark. The main door alone was accessible and the porters kept that closely watched; there was always the Fellows' Gate, but it required a special key.

"She might well remain within college," Orlando suggested, "and could be smoked out, even now."

"A lady may have been here, gentlemen," Dr. Peters suddenly looked very uncomfortable, "but I'm not so deeply immersed in the groves of academe as some of my colleagues and I do understand the nature of the things that can go on in a single sex society. It's just possible that this is still a *crime of passion* and there be no woman involved."

The doctor arrived very soon afterwards and expressed the opinion that Lord Morcar had been dead for perhaps one or two hours. He spoke quietly with the Master, while the two younger fellows shivered in the draught from the window. They envied the sense their superior had shown in putting on a heavy cloak before venturing out and both thought with regret about the cozy fireside they'd been forced to abandon. The older men carried on their conversation, heads bowed, faces serious, until Peters turned to them. "Gentlemen, I needn't tell you that it would be best for the college if you were not to mention what you've seen here to anyone."

"But the police, sir." Orlando ventured, no doubt for the first time in his career, to query the Master's instructions. "Surely we'll be required to give them all assistance?"

"The police yes, Dr. Coppersmith, but no one else. I will not have this whispered abroad at Hall—neither at St. Bride's nor at any other college. Do I make myself clear?"

"Amply so, sir." It was Stewart who made the reply, lightly touching Orlando's arm in case the man should see fit to make another uncharacteristic challenge to the authorities. Was the world to turn completely upside down

Lessons in Love

this night?

As if answering some prepared cue, heavy-booted footsteps on the stairs announced the arrival of the constabulary. Peters and Coppersmith knew one of the bowler-hatted gentlemen—Inspector Wilson, who'd successfully dealt with a series of audacious burglaries committed at St. Bride's the previous summer. Wilson raised his hat to the company and introduced his colleague, Sergeant Cohen. The Inspector easily 'passed for a gentleman' as the old saying went, which was the very reason why he was always sent to deal with university business, even if the crimes were sometimes below what his rank warranted. The Sergeant seemed to be almost a Gilbert and Sullivan caricature of what a policeman of *his* rank should be—big, bluff and extremely competent in a slow, methodical way.

Now it was the turn of these men to go into a huddle with Dr. Peters and the doctor, leaving Stewart and Coppersmith to shiver again. Once or twice they became aware, from glances and nods, that their role in this affair was being mentioned.

Eventually Wilson came over and addressed them. "Gentlemen, have you moved or touched anything in this room since you first arrived here?" When he seemed satisfied that the answer to both was *no*, he resumed, "then you may return to your rooms. I'll need to talk to both of you tomorrow."

The two young men readily agreed, desperate both for warmth and to get out of the same room as that pale, sad body. They soon began their cold trek back to Orlando's set of rooms.

"There's some of that bottle left, Dr. Stewart, if you need something to keep out the cold." Coppersmith raised an eyebrow in silent plea and his friend nodded his willingness to comply.

"I think that I'm beyond keeping out the cold but I might be able to persuade it to vacate the premises." Jonty managed a grin, something Orlando could never have done, given the circumstances.

They didn't speak a word as they crossed the courtyard, making the most of the fellows' privilege of walking on the grass, despite the snow, which now lay an inch or two deep. The glasses they'd left half empty they now refilled.

"Here you are, Jonty, drive out the chill with this." Orlando thrust a generous measure of port into Stewart's hand. It was strange and endearing that Coppersmith had reverted to using his Christian name the minute they'd entered the set of rooms again.

"Thank you, Orlando—it's been a long night and I guess this is just the beginning of many long days." Jonty sipped the excellent vintage appreciatively and studied his companion. Coppersmith looked a broken man. It must have been a great shock to him that his nice little academic world had been sullied by something as common and grubby as a strangling. And this had followed directly after his nice little academic world being sullied by a spark of something else—desire, attraction, lust? Who knew what name to give it, but it had been there.

It would have been the easiest thing in the world for Stewart to go over, sit on the arm of Orlando's chair and put his arm around the man's shoulders. It certainly would have been simple twenty-four hours ago, but not now—not after whatever strange electricity had crackled between them in this very room a few hours ago. He settled for walking across and clapping Coppersmith on the back. "I'll see you tomorrow. No, later today I suppose it would be." He moved to the door, "Will you be all right?" What he meant was *would you like me to stay?* but that particular thought remained unspoken.

"I'll be fine, thank you, Jonty." Coppersmith produced a wan smile. "Thank you for your help tonight—thank you for everything."

Lessons in Love

"Do you think it's a crime of passion, Orlando?" It was afternoon and Stewart had found himself for the third time in twenty four hours admitted to the inner sanctum of Dr. Coppersmith's rooms. That after weeks of not even being allowed to view this hallowed area from around the door. It was almost as if his friend, once resolved that Jonty wasn't going to commit any act as disgraceful as the one that had caused their meeting, had accepted that it was perfectly acceptable for this man to be allowed to grace his chambers. They were taking a cup of tea and sharing Chelsea buns, buns that were sticky and oozing with fruit.

"Crime of passion?" Coppersmith seemed to be having trouble grasping the concept.

Jonty shook his head and wondered. *Perhaps he simply doesn't have any definition of what passion is?* Stewart had noticed that, in all their conversations, there'd never been any hint that Orlando had even kissed another person, with the exception of his much lamented mother. But then Jonty had never given his friend the slightest intimation that *he* had any experience of the romance which he studied so avidly in the works of the Bard. Romeo and Juliet. Troilus and Cressida. Antonio and Bassanio. *Yes, well that last pairing might be a better approximation of the truth.* If Dr. Stewart spoke so authoritatively to his students about the early sonnets, it was because he had practical knowledge to apply.

Jonty became impatient waiting for an answer to his question. "Yes, *crime of passion*, surely you must understand what I mean by it. Have you never read *Othello*? Or even the *News of the World*? It would amount to the same thing in this case."

If Coppersmith was struggling with *crime of passion*, he seemed totally flummoxed by *News of the World*. "I'm sorry, Jonty, my father never allowed such reading matter in our home."

"Oh, for goodness sake!" Stewart went over to the window and made a great point of studying the court. The fresh snow had obliterated their footsteps over the grass from the previous night, but now the flurries had stopped and the sky was clearing. *Hard frost tonight; no comfort in the weather and none in all the world for that poor young man's family.* Jonty's attention was grabbed by the appearance of two bowler-hatted men. Wilson and Cohen were making their way towards Coppersmith's staircase and obviously their interrogation was imminent.

The policemen were polite to a fault, but their questions were penetrating and the two fellows of St. Bride's were sure that any uncertainty in their answers would be seized on. Jonty in particular felt like one of the students facing a grueling tutorial—one of Coppersmith's, probably. The 'tutorial' focused first and foremost on the chronology of the previous night's events and the observations that the two young men had made. Inspector Wilson asked the questions, with Cohen taking copious notes and producing the occasional incisive remark. The second element was to establish whether anyone could have gained access to or from St. Bride's using either of the men's keys for the Fellows' Gate and they drew a resounding negative here.

The third theme concerned Lord Morcar's personal life. Although Coppersmith had been able to produce frighteningly exact and plentiful observations about the evening before, he seemed to have little to offer about this subject. Stewart had, though. He'd spent part of the night— too tired to sleep, brain whirling—considering what he knew about the victim and how much he should disclose. In the end he'd decided that complete honesty, while potentially painful to the memory of the young man, was the only proper course.

"I have things to say that I hope will be treated with the utmost confidence. If they were to be spoken of outside these walls, they might cause enormous distress to Lord Morcar's family." Receiving reassurance that the police would use their discretion at all times, he continued. "As I understand it from what I've heard, this lad's romantic tastes were what would be called unusual. I doubt if you'll come across a young lady in this case, but young men in plenty you may well find."

Wilson raised an eyebrow. "And you have evidence for this, Dr. Stewart?"

"Only that of my own ears and eyes. I knew of Lord Morcar before I returned to St. Bride's—I was at University College in London and sometimes met his brother at my club. He got rather deep in his cups one night and began to tell me his worries over his younger sibling's proclivities. There'd been some minor scandal with one of the grooms, I understand. I didn't encourage him to say more, he would only have hated both himself and me afterwards. I simply got him even more drunk and succeeded in making him forget he'd said anything at all."

Stewart stole a glance at Dr. Coppersmith—the man was looking both embarrassed and perplexed. Steeling his nerve, Jonty carried on. "When I came here a month ago, I discovered that Lord Morcar had come up last year. I must admit that what little I saw of his interactions with his fellow students confirmed what I'd been told. Not just his conduct in college, I hasten to add—I've seen him on two occasions in the town with young men who would be termed 'ladies of easy virtue' were they female."

"And do you have proof that these young men were what you say they were?"

"I don't, but I saw plenty of the type in London—they're very common in certain parts of the city. And one of the other English fellows warned me that there were places here to be avoided should you not want to run the risk of being accosted. I would be surprised if you don't know where I mean. Perhaps it would be profitable to enquire there."

"I'm pleased that you have such useful advice to offer us, sir." The bite in the Sergeant's voice was evident, but the Inspector interrupted him.

"I do know of these places, Dr. Stewart, and I will be

enquiring there. You've nothing further to add?" Wilson fixed the man with a very piercing look.

"I don't. I've told you everything I know and it's cost my conscience greatly, retelling what was told to me by a man so much the worse for brandy that he wasn't aware of what he said." The consternation on Jonty's face was plain and the policemen quickly concluded the interview.

By now the tea was cold and the cakes turning stale and the two fellows sat in silence, considering all that had been said. Coppersmith broke the mood by leaping to his feet. "We risk being late for high table, Jonty." He reached for his gown, but was forestalled by a hand on his arm.

"Not tonight, Orlando. I had a word with the Master this afternoon and suggested that you might need a bit of quiet to recover from the shocks of yesterday. I hinted that some of the fellows might be indiscreet enough to want to venture a question or two and that we would be best out of the college for the evening." Stewart grinned. "I'm glad to say he agreed."

Coppersmith looked absolutely stunned. Jonty knew he'd dined in college almost every night of the last six years and the thought that there could be other acceptable venues might well be alien to him. "But where will we eat? We've no invitation to another college." Orlando had received some of those in his first year at St. Bride's, but his taciturnity at table had ensured that they hadn't been repeated.

Jonty rolled his eyes, a habitual act that usually preceded an exclamation of surprise. "Orlando, I've known you months and you still have the capacity to amaze me. We can eat at The Bishop's Cope; it's only ten minutes walk at the most."

Blank incomprehension greeted Stewart's suggestion and he fought hard not to snort. *Has this man spent the last six years with his eyes and ears closed? Does he have no perception of the world outside these walls?*

"The Bishop's Cope, Orlando—it was an excellent pub

in my student years and I've had the chance to test it again with some of the chaps from the School of English. It may not have the dignity of Hall, and you'll get some strange looks if you insist on having the grace in Latin before your steak and kidney pie, but the food is glorious and the beer a poem." He hauled on his coat and motioned Coppersmith to do the same. "Come on, the novelty will do you the world of good!" And, so saying, he dragged his friend out into the icy evening.

Jonty had been right. The food at The Bishop's Cope turned out to be hot, tasty and in splendid quantities. The two men could only manage the barest soupcon of apple pie for pudding before admitting defeat. They stretched their legs and enjoyed the warmth of the fire.

"Did you have a favorite pub in Oxford, Coppersmith? I always loved this one, and The Mackerel, when we weren't in disgrace with the landlord."

"I rarely went to any pubs, Stewart. Always too much studying to be done."

Jonty slammed his pint onto the table. "And you a rugby player! Surely you allowed yourself a bit of refreshment after a match?"

Orlando sipped his beer pensively. "Sometimes, certainly—but not habitually." He sighed and looked around him at the glowing pots and friendly faces. "Perhaps I made the wrong decision."

Jonty clapped him on the arm. "Never too late to learn to appreciate life's pleasures. Let Dr. Stewart lead you astray." He laughed and finished his beer.

Coppersmith considered his friend carefully. There had been some scant hint in the last remarks that he couldn't work out. It reminded him of what had happened the previous evening before the porter knocked the door, that fluttering sensation in the pit of his stomach, and he couldn't fathom that out, either, despite applying all his powers of logic. He drained his glass and rose, reluctant to face the cold night but wary of taking in too much more of the excellent ale.

They sauntered back to college, Stewart admiring the beautifully clear sky and Coppersmith clandestinely admiring his beautiful companion. For he'd concluded that, as certainly as opposite over adjacent gives the tangent, Dr. Stewart was the most beautiful thing he'd ever seen—it was an unspoken and immutable law.

They entered St. Bride's by the main gate, respectfully greeted by Summerbee, who seemed to change his face from one of disapproval on realizing that the people entering were legitimately allowed to be out and about. He was no doubt slightly disappointed, as the porters' lodge was said to be holding a sweepstake on who could catch the most miscreants or intruders. Jonty speculated, under his breath, whether the man needed to increase his score.

The snow had frozen hard on the paths through the Old Court and the friends skidded most of the way along, Stewart giggling as he went. They felt light headed from lack of sleep and excess of ale and simply wanted to assert the wonderful feeling of being alive, even in the face of recent tragedy. "Got some excellent port in my rooms, Coppersmith. Glass or two would set you up for a good night's sleep. What do you say?"

"I don't think I'd better, Stewart. I have a lecture to give tomorrow and need a clear head." Orlando didn't look like he had an entirely lucid head at the moment—beer and emotion no doubt vying with one another. He must have noticed the fleeting disappointment on his friend's face and seemed to be making an effort to think clearly. "Cup of coffee might be a good idea—hot and strong."

"Cup of coffee it is, then."

Jonty's room was a complete contrast to Orlando's. Messy, cozy, welcoming, pictures of the seemingly limitless

Lessons in Love

Stewart family abounding. Coppersmith poked the fire into life and found a comfortable seat at one end of a sofa. Coffee soon appeared. Jonty poured two cups and settled down next to his friend. They didn't talk, they didn't feel the need of it but simply drank and mused on their own thoughts, surreptitiously taking glances at each other and enjoying the sight.

"Orlando," it was the merest whisper from Stewart, "I do value your friendship. Enormously. I suspect that there are times when you find me frivolous or annoying, but I do hope that we'll always remain close." He wanted to risk a touch, to find that electricity again which had arced between them the night before but he was too afraid that the moment had been lost forever.

"And I hope so too, Jonty. You're the only real friend I've ever had and I know that I exasperate you, too, but I treasure the day that you came and stole my chair and every single day since." Coppersmith smiled, something that Jonty felt he did more often, the more time they spent together.

Jonty's smile in response was tender and affectionate, a great wave of warmth swelling in his chest. "I never stole your chair—I was simply borrowing it until I was allowed one of my own." Stewart reached his arm across, laying his hand lightly on his friend's. "Always want to sit in the chair next to yours, Orlando." He gently squeezed the hand that lay beneath his, felt a slight answering pressure and made his own grip tighter. He felt the same tingling of excitement as when their hands had touched before.

"Is this what Morcar did, Jonty?" The question rang like a pistol shot, breaking the mood and making Stewart start.

"I beg your pardon, Orlando?"

"Morcar, is this what he did with his men—hold hands?" Coppersmith's dark brown eyes were full of unasked questions and Stewart felt incredibly touched by the sight of them. His fingers closed tighter over his friend's hands, feeling the trembling that had to be a signal of either excitement or fear.

"Well, I guess so. Hold hands, kiss, caress, all sorts of different things, you know."

Coppersmith obviously didn't know, hadn't the first idea. Jonty was sure that he would be feeling confused at the events of the previous night, both the murder and the tentative romance. "And was there more? For it to have ended in his death, I mean. Would anyone be killed for a caress?"

Stewart weighed his words carefully; he wasn't sure what was going on in Orlando's head and the last thing he wanted to do was scare the man away. "Men have been betrayed to their death with a kiss, but I doubt that anyone would be killed for something so trivial." He took one glance at Coppersmith and realized that his friend didn't regard any kiss as trivial. "There may have been more, Orlando," Jonty sighed and carried on. It seemed heartbreaking to have to knock some of the wonderful ingenuousness out of such an innocent. "Men do lie with men, as men do with women. The processes are, I understand, not entirely dissimilar."

Coppersmith nodded, as if adding more points to a particular theorem, one that was an unfamiliar mix of facts and emotion. "What if I wished to kiss you, Jonty? I feel the need of it so very much and yet even I know that it would break the laws of both society and the church. I wonder whether it would spoil our friendship or if it would make our bond of comradeship stronger?"

Stewart felt an irrational wave of anger at such clinical analysis; he was sorely tempted to strike his friend out of sheer frustration. Breaking their handclasp, he strode over to the fireplace, beating the mantelpiece with his fists, instead. "Your powers of examination show great credit to your academic ability, but must you evaluate *everything*, Orlando? If you want to kiss me, come over here and do it. If not, I rather think that I'd prefer you to leave." He shut his eyes, bowing his head onto the ledge, unable to bear the

Lessons in Love

inevitable sight of Coppersmith going through the door. They'd reached a crux and he was certain he'd mishandled the whole affair.

To his great astonishment, he felt his face being lifted by strong hands and lips being lightly pressed to his forehead, to his cheek, his forehead again. "May I?" Brown eyes looked from blue eyes to red lips, back to blue eyes. Coppersmith hadn't left—perhaps at last he'd realized what he had to do and was determined to see it through.

Jonty's skin tingled beneath his friend's fingers. "But of course, Orlando." Stewart began to relax again.

Coppersmith tentatively leaned forward, brushed Jonty's lips and cheeks with his own lips. A puzzled expression on Orlando's face broke the spell. "I didn't realize your cheeks would be quite as rough, Jonty."

Stewart snorted. "Well what did you expect, Orlando—a baby's bottom? Shall I go strop my razor and shave?" His wide grin lit up his handsome face and Coppersmith smiled shyly in return, looking for all the world like a little boy who'd found a shilling.

"No. It was merely an observation, I don't find it unpleasant." Orlando brushed his lips up against Jonty's again, then drew him into a close embrace, the two of them drinking in the wonderful scents of soap and sweat. He leaned down to make another attempt at a kiss but was forestalled by loud footsteps and voices outside in the court and then on the stairs.

"If they knock on my door we must pretend not to be here," Stewart whispered, with something like desperation in his voice. It was too cruel to be interrupted twice running, especially when it had taken so long to break down Orlando's reserve.

"We can't, you know. They'll see the light under the door." The inevitable knock came. "You must answer." Coppersmith took a final, swift embrace. "I'm sorry."

"So am I, Orlando." Jonty ran his fingers down the beloved face of his friend, savoring the smooth skin and tender lips. They broke their hold and Stewart opened the door.

He was confronted by a second year student called Trumper, whom he suspected had a bit of a crush on him, the same student who'd helped clear the stairwell the night before. Trumper had another young man by the arm. "This is Jackson, Dr. Stewart. He found Douglas'—I mean Lord Morcar's—body, last night. He has something to show you." Trumper tightened his grip on the man by his side and thrust him forward.

"Think it might be best not to do this out here," whispered Jackson.

Reluctantly Jonty admitted them. They showed no surprise at finding Coppersmith in occupation, probably because the man seemed to have his nose in a dusty historical tome.

Trumper spoke again. "Someone," he indicated Jackson, "wasn't entirely honest with the police today. Said he hadn't touched or taken anything from the room but he had. Show them."

Jackson produced a piece of paper from his pocket. "It was lying on...on the body. I only went to Douglas' room to borrow some ink, I forgot to get some yesterday, and I found him." The lad started to shiver. "He was dead. This note was on his chest."

"Don't touch it, Stewart." Coppersmith produced his commanding voice again. "Have none of you heard of fingerprints? Jackson, as you've already touched the paper, you must lay it on the table if you wish us to look at it. Thank you."

They all perused the sheet, horror growing with each word read.

"AS SODOM AND GOMORRAH PERISHED SO MUST YOU. YOU ARE AN ABOMINATION."

"Dear God," whispered Stewart, turning to Coppersmith, who was deathly white. Their whole world had turned to utter chaos.

Chapter Three

The next day the wind backed to the south and brought a thaw all over East Anglia. Students deprived of their snowball fights and skating on frozen fields returned with reluctance to their studies. Even St. Bride's was showing every sign of normal life, despite the continuing and deepening enquiries into the young mathematics scholar's death. Dr. Stewart had marched Jackson and Trumper straight to the Police Station first thing in the morning, and it *was* first thing, eight o'clock out the door being a distinct shock to their systems. He'd found Sergeant Cohen and made the two lads explain the whole sorry tale. The paper, now safe from contamination within a large envelope—Coppersmith's suggestion—was produced and examined.

Cohen was even harder on the students than he'd been on Jonty the day before. "You do understand the serious nature of withholding evidence from the police?" They did. "Then what possessed you to do it?"

Jackson's voice reverted to the cracked treble of his pubertal years, not long past. "It was the thought of the shame it might bring on his family. I hoped that you would think that he'd been killed by a burglar—or a woman."

Stewart wondered whether this thought had suddenly appeared in Jackson's vapid brain and whether he was rather proud of it. He rolled his eyes at Cohen and, to his surprise, saw a kindred look of slightly amused exasperation in those green eyes. *I think I could grow to like this man—if I ever had the chance to talk to him outside of an inquisition chamber.* "Sergeant Cohen, I think all present here agree that Jackson has acted like the worst kind of idiot, but I for one don't believe that he has any further involvement in this matter. I'm grateful to Mr. Trumper for knocking some sense into his foolish brain and I only wish that they'd brought the evidence straight to you last night, but I suspect the small matter of a porter's lodge full of eagle-eyed jailers rather inhibited them."

"I dare say you're right on the second count, sir, but I'll reserve judgment on your first point for the moment." Cohen carefully left the paper for Inspector Wilson to peruse and showed them to the door. "And if you find any other evidence, it will be left in place, won't it?" The two sheepish young lads nodded their heads and departed.

"Thank you, Dr. Stewart," Cohen held out his hand. "I appreciate that the situation will become more difficult for St. Bride's with the appearance of this note, but we must continue our investigations rigorously. I'm very much afraid that this won't be just an isolated killing. Where mania is concerned, they rarely are."

Stewart shook hands and departed, chilled more now than he'd ever been on Monday night in that little, draughty room.

Jonty didn't see Orlando again until they took sherry together in the Senior Common Room before dinner. The room was abuzz with talk—despite the Master's best efforts, the details of the circumstances concerning Morcar's death had begun to become common knowledge and there was even a disquieting rumor that a note had been

Lessons in Love

found that was somehow connected to the crime.

Wilson and Cohen had been straight to see Dr. Peters with the letter and had subsequently been asking questions of all the fellows, questions not just concerning the keys to the Fellows' Gate. The police were rapidly forming the view that the assailant had come from and remained within St. Bride's, something that would bring even more distress to the Master. But even he wouldn't be able to deny that it was highly unlikely for a stranger to have evaded the notice of the porters or have scaled any of the gates or walls.

Lumley, the chaplain, seemed particularly hurt that the police had subjected him to such an arduous examination. "The things they asked me, Dr. Coppersmith, about whether I'd any personal knowledge of that unfortunate young man, they stopped barely short of asking me if I'd heard the boy's confession at any point. Then to ask whether I had any particular insight into religious mania, was aware of any in St. Bride's, or had come across any such thing before. And some of the things they hinted were going on within the environs of this university—I like to think that I'm fairly well acquainted with the world, but I was certainly horrified and you would have been, too!"

Jonty successfully repressed a snigger. He'd known the chaplain during his earlier time at the college and *well acquainted with the world* the man was not. As for what went on within the 'environs'—Stewart could have told him things that would have made his eyeballs jump out of their sockets and rotate.

The indignation among the fellows gradually diminished during an excellent dinner, helped by some rather good college hock. By the time that they took coffee and fruit in the SCR, the topics of conversation had generally returned to planarian worms, the nature of electrons and other mundane items such as were suitable for men of learning to entertain themselves with.

"And what have you been up to today, Coppersmith?" The two rightful backsides occupied the two chairs in the corner this evening. Orlando had inspected the upholstery of his very closely, Jonty wondering all the while whether he was looking to see if a very small female had hidden herself under the antimacassar.

He'd been worrying about Orlando pretty well continuously since they'd separated the previous night. Having agreed that he'd accompany the two students to the Police station, Stewart had at last persuaded them to leave and he wanted the opportunity of making sure that this latest blow hadn't overwhelmed his friend. But Coppersmith had been icily calm, dealing with the shock by retreating into himself. They'd said goodnight and parted, as if nothing of significance had happened between them. Jonty was frightened that *nothing of significance* would ever happen between them again.

He tried the light-hearted approach. "You've got a rather smug look trying to escape from under your usual frown. You may be able to fool the rest of the college but I've come to know you too well—you have a secret."

Coppersmith lowered his voice and leant over confidentially. "Inspector Wilson visited me today; he had a particular request to make." Orlando looked around furtively, as if to ensure that they weren't being overheard, but the other fellows were talking about parthenogenesis, which was a bit racy and kept them all occupied. "He asked whether I, we, could use our knowledge of St. Bride's to help in the investigation."

Stewart wrinkled his little nose. "Did he actually mean that we should use our eyes and ears to spy upon our fellow college members? Well, don't look so shocked. Wilson and Cohen are very astute men and I wouldn't for a moment put it past them to want to gain access to inside information. And they're not going to get it from the chaplain, are they?"

Coppersmith smirked then quickly hid it. "I think that a little private investigation may have been the intended result. I've been trying to oblige them." He looked exceedingly self-satisfied and Stewart could barely restrain

Lessons in Love

himself from thumping him. Or kissing him. Either would have done.

"I think that I should deliberately not ask you what you mean by that, just to punish you."

Coppersmith snorted, "I'd tell you anyway, irrespective of whether you pretended not to want to be told. I know you rather well, too." Their eyes met briefly, then passed on to safer sights—the reality of what had nearly happened the last two evenings was too raw between them. They had been so close to sharing their affection and the repeated interruptions had led to awkwardness. "I've been searching my memories of the past six years to find if there's been anything at St. Bride's that might relate to this matter."

"And is there something?" Stewart looked like an eager hound that had just caught the merest hint of the scent.

"Nothing whatsoever."

"Oh." Jonty's disappointment was displayed all over his handsome face. He'd been sure that his brilliant friend was going to make some revelation that would easily lead to the solution of this case. He felt rather cheated.

"But that tells us something in itself, Dr. Stewart. It probably means that the culprit, assuming the police are right in believing that he is from within the college and I agree with them there, must be a relative newcomer." He fixed his friend with an unconvincingly fierce gaze. "It's not you, is it?"

Jonty looked rather shocked, not at the accusation but at the fact that his friend had suddenly taken to making almost frivolous remarks. *Perhaps the last two evenings are having a positive effect upon him.* Encouraged, he snorted and mustered a reply. "Dr. Coppersmith, I'm one of the few people with an impeccable alibi, having been in your company the whole evening. But I think that you've made a presumption too far in your deductions. You might still be looking for someone who has been here a while; people do suddenly change and manifest strange behavior, perhaps as a result of some trauma or great upheaval in their lives. You might do so, if I ever got the chance to kiss you properly."

Orlando froze, eyeing the company as if worried they'd been overheard. All must have seemed safe, so he hissed, "Watch what you say, Stewart. There are too many eyes peering into the doings of St. Bride's for you to risk the chance of our activities being too closely scrutinized."

Jonty felt his hackles rising, "Didn't seem to bother you last night, Dr. Coppersmith, when it was all *may I kiss you, Jonty?* Dare say it would have been *may I come into your bed, Jonty?* if we hadn't been interrupted." The silence following this remark was louder than gun-fire. Stewart realized, too late, far too late, that he'd said far too much. It was his own thoughts that had turned to that small bed last night; he suspected Orlando hadn't even let a carnal thought cross his mind. Not last night, not ever.

Coppersmith now sat unmoving, looking at his friend with horror. Suddenly rising, he swept from the Senior Common Room, his gown moving behind him like the great tail of some large, angry, black dog. The fellows stared after him in amazement, then exchanged knowing looks with one another.

Jonty guessed that his colleagues were discussing him and his friend—*a quarrel, it had to happen one day with a man such as Coppersmith, it's a wonder that Stewart has prevented it happening up to now.* He took a dignified departure but couldn't return to his rooms as too many painful memories lay there, so decided to take a turn about the town. *How could I have been so idiotic?* He strode up to King's Parade then down again, oblivious to everything around him, seeing only with his mind's eye, watching the events of two days replayed again and again. *He will never forgive me.*

Jonty wandered along to Trumpington Street, round past the conduit and back along Tennis Court Road, muttering to himself all the time. He was coming out of School Lane when he heard a familiar and most welcome voice. "Dr. Stewart, what are you doing?" A tall, rangy figure stepped into the pool of light under the street lamp. "I called at your rooms but you weren't there—the porters said that you'd gone out. I was so worried about you—hadn't the slightest idea where you'd gone." The distress in Orlando's voice was plain, heaping further guilt on Jonty's conscience.

"I just needed to think, Dr. Coppersmith." An irritated thought crossed Stewart's mind. "You didn't imagine that I'd thrown myself off a bridge somewhere, lovelorn and heartbroken?" He could feel his hackles rising, a tight knot of anger in his stomach.

"I did not! I could envisage you going to The Bishop's Cope and getting the worse for drink—that was the first place I checked—but I never considered you idiotic enough to kill yourself." Even by the dim street lamp's light, with the mist drifting over from the river, Orlando looked intensely worried. "You didn't contemplate it, did you?"

Stewart snorted, his anger beginning to ebb away in the face of Coppersmith's concern. "For about fifty-seven seconds, yes. Then I decided that it would give me more satisfaction to live on and cause further nuisance to you. I've decided to make it my life's ambition to be a constant pest to mathematics fellows. You will be just the first of many." Jonty grinned, one of his puckish grins that he used to twist his mother around his finger. Orlando murmured something indistinct.

"You'll have to speak up, Orlando. If that's how you lecture your students, I wonder that any of them can understand a word of what you say." Stewart grinned again; he bet that the students didn't understand a word of Coppersmith's lectures anyway, even if they heard every syllable.

"Don't want there to be any others than me, Jonty." Orlando's gaze seemed to be fixed on a particularly interesting paving stone. He looked intensely embarrassed to be discussing such things out in the street.

"Then why all the remonstrating against what I said in the Senior Common Room and the caution about *our activities being too closely scrutinized?* Weren't you trying to warn me off?"

"Of course not, although I was slightly alarmed at how freely you spoke there." Coppersmith kept his gaze fixed on the pavement. "We should be having this conversation back in your rooms."

Stewart grunted. "I doubt if the members of the SCR would notice if I stripped naked and leapt in your lap, unless you were sitting in the wrong chair, of course. I might try it tomorrow night."

"We are dining at St. Thomas' tomorrow night, so you can't..." Orlando stopped, making Jonty suppress a smile at the man's beloved logic having let him down. Coppersmith raised his head, sighed, and appeared to relax. "I was only concerned for your safety—our safety. I didn't mean that the fellows were necessarily observing us, nor even the police. There's a maniac at St. Bride's, Dr. Stewart, Inspector Wilson is sure of it, and he's preyed on one young man who showed too great a liking for his own sex. What if he turned his attention to us?"

Jonty was genuinely surprised. He understood that the madman who had killed Lord Morcar would possibly strike again, but it had never occurred to him that he and Orlando were putting themselves into the position of potential victims. "But he would never know, Coppersmith."

"He knew about Morcar, although it seems that very few other people did." Orlando put his hand on his friend's arm, the first time they had touched since the embraces of the previous evening. "I never set much worth on my life before, but now I have reason to value it." The grip on Stewart's arm tightened. "The last forty-eight hours have been a great strain upon me, emotionally draining, physically exciting," Orlando's voice had dropped to a whisper, "and now I would never want to see you hurt."

The words had been spoken and could not be retrieved, deepest thoughts revealed and the risk taken of being spurned. Jonty laid his own hand lightly over the one on his

Lessons in Love

arm. "My dearest friend. If it means so much to you, then we'll remain no closer than associates until the college is free of this villain." He broke their contact and smiled shyly. "And when the perpetrator is caught, then such times we'll have, Coppersmith. Such times."

Orlando shifted his feet. "Jonty, you know I have no idea what *such times* might involve but if you're in charge, then I feel safe. Villain in the college or not."

They returned to St. Bride's in silence, so much unsaid but needing no words this or any night. They parted, with just a manly handshake, inside the gates and returned to sets of rooms that had never seemed lonely before but now felt strangely lacking in something or other.

The next morning the college was abuzz with rumor. *Someone has confessed to the murder, he's been arrested by the police, he's in court at this very moment.* Once the truth had been dissected from the flesh of supposition, it turned out that one of the third year historians had indeed made a confession. The young man had walked voluntarily into the police station that morning and, or so the Master told his colleagues, was being questioned by Inspector Wilson. Everyone in St. Bride's was extremely grateful that the cloud over the college had been so swiftly lifted.

Stewart was grateful, too. Now he could look forward to a sumptuous dinner at St. Thomas' that night and just the smallest possibility, no bigger than a man's hand, of some more romantic activity with the man currently sitting to his left. He risked a very small sidelong glance, but Coppersmith's stern face revealed nothing. *Well, we shall see.*

It was dark that evening along by the river, dark and icy. The Cam had suffered greatly from the melting snow and had rather inconsiderately burst its banks and then

37

frozen over. The route along to the back of the college from St. Thomas' was treacherous and the two men had to cling together over some stretches. Stewart seemed to find this whole episode hilarious and they wound up at the Fellows' Gate in a shocking state. Coppersmith mustered the resolve to open the lock in a dignified fashion, let them both in and very carefully relocked it. Everyone at St. Bride's was becoming extra cautious now, even though the culprit appeared to be in custody.

They crossed the Fellows' Garden arm in arm, frost crackling beneath their feet. Suddenly Jonty stopped, raising his finger to his lips. They were in the deep shadow of one of the trees, black shades against the night, hardly able to see each other, let alone be seen by anyone else. Stewart pulled at the arm linked into his, drawing Coppersmith closer until they were face-to-face, chest-to-chest, breath coming rapidly and not just because of the cold.

"Little bit of unfinished business to attend to, Coppersmith." His strong fingers stroked down Orlando's face and touched cold lips.

Coppersmith could feel the fluttering sensations—those strange little vibrations that always appeared when he was close to Jonty—dancing in his stomach again. "Out here, Stewart? Anyone could come along."

"Ah, but they won't, will they? Dare to venture out on this treacherous ice, I mean. And there are no doors here for people to pound on and interrupt us. There'll be no interruptions at all this time." And at last Jonty managed to give his friend a real kiss. No simple brushing of lips as there'd been in his rooms, this time it was a full and lasting contact, sweet and tender.

Coppersmith savored the taste of what was his first proper kiss. He'd been trying for days to imagine what it would be like and he'd, inevitably, got it entirely wrong. "That was astonishing, really very..." Orlando was silenced by a finger raised to his mouth.

"Analyzing again, Coppersmith. You must stop it."

Lessons in Love

Jonty gave him another kiss, longer and even fuller this time. "There's nothing to evaluate here, Orlando, just relax and enjoy what we have." He tried a third kiss, this one with the merest hint of his tongue touching Coppersmith's lips.

"Stewart, what are you doing?" Coppersmith was alarmed. This he hadn't expected at all and he wasn't sure it was right.

"Well, this is how we must learn to kiss, unless you're intending we pretend to be a very old married couple who have no further use for passion. Stop thinking. Simply do what feels right." A fourth kiss felt right; a very long kiss, accompanied by an extended embrace, head against head, Jonty's arm caressing Orlando's shoulders.

A fifth kiss deepened, this time Coppersmith decided that perhaps it was acceptable to do this strange thing, to form such an intimate liaison with someone you had a great affection for. He tried probing a little bit with his own tongue and it proved a surprisingly pleasant thing to do. Orlando eventually broke the hold, gasping for breath. "I never even imagined it would be like this, Jonty, not once. What have I been missing all my life?"

"Me, of course, you great oaf. I think that if I hadn't come and *stolen your chair*, as you persist in alleging, you would never have kissed anyone."

"You presume a great deal, Stewart. I might still have blossomed into the sort of man who would have gone about kissing almost anybody, with or without your influence."

"Perhaps I do presume, Coppersmith. Perhaps I've made the untoward assumption that you find me, alone of anyone you've ever met, irresistible. So irresistible that you're desperate to come back to my rooms for a hot, strong coffee despite the supervision you have to dispense to the dunderheads tomorrow morning."

"None of my students are dunderheads. The entrance examination ensures that idiots go straight to study English, or failing that to the School of Agriculture."

"Too cold to argue out here—let's get the kettle on."

Arm in arm again, they walked contentedly out of the garden and towards Middle Court, full of anticipation at what might happen once they reached Stewart's rooms. They heard the first hints of commotion as they passed through the archway; raised voices, scuffling feet, a hint of rising panic in the air. Then they saw Lee, the porter, running in the direction of the Master's lodge, and a crowd of students around the entrance to a staircase.

"Not again, Coppersmith. It can't be, surely." Stewart looked confused and frightened. They had all assumed that they were now safe, that St. Bride's had been rid of the menace once and for all. They strode over to the melee, where Summerbee now stood guard. He nodded to the fellows, showing relief at the arrival of the cavalry.

"Dr. Coppersmith, Dr. Stewart, there's been another..." he seemed to search for a suitable word, "occurrence, sir."

"And who is it this time?" Orlando's voice sounded like each word he spoke was made of ice and steel. He felt chilled to the bone to hear the contrast in his own voice to the tender phrases he'd so recently spoken.

"Russell-Clarke—he's a Physics scholar, sir—I mean he *was* a Physics scholar. Nice lad, very quiet but always polite to us and a case of beer for the porters' lodge at Christmas."

"Would you like us to go up and take a look?" Coppersmith glanced at Jonty, who nodded his agreement.

"Yes, if you would be so kind, sir. The chaplain's up there at the moment, saying a few words over him. It was the chaplain who discovered the body." Lee lowered his voice. "Says that Mr. Russell-Clarke had left a note that he wanted to talk to him, private like. When Dr. Lumley went to see him, he found..."

"Thank you, Lee," Stewart tapped the man on the shoulder, "it's not an easy task to deal with. You're doing a grand job." They reluctantly mounted the stairs, entering the room to find the chaplain as pale as the body he was standing by, with his eyes closed and his soft voice

Lessons in Love

murmuring prayers. Stewart bowed his head in genuine reverence and Coppersmith followed suit.

All three men opened their eyes together when the orisons ended. The first things Orlando looked for were telltale bruising on the neck and disheveled clothes—they were both present—and the window was open, too. The note lay beside the body this time, probably swept there by the breeze. Identical words, identical style, evidence of the same insane hand.

The chaplain began to cry and Jonty put his arm around the man's shoulders. "It's not just the scandalous taking of life that unnerves me, Dr. Stewart, it's the blasphemy. To associate such an act with Holy Scripture—it is wicked, truly wicked."

"Amen to that, Lumley," Jonty replied, and Coppersmith knew he meant every word.

Chapter Four

Dr. Jonty Stewart, fellow of St. Bride's, lay in his bed without sleeping. Another evening that had promised much had slipped through his fingers. True, the time in the Fellows' garden had been wonderful, but life seemed determined to prevent anything more exquisite from occurring between him and his *mathematical friend*, as the chaplain referred to Coppersmith.

The chaplain; poor Lumley, he'd been so shattered at discovering the second body that Stewart had offered to stay with him until first the Master and then the police had arrived. And then he'd remained again throughout the length of their questioning. Lumley had found enough strength to answer all questions lucidly and logically.

He'd told them that he'd seen Russell-Clarke in the chapel early that morning. The young man had been very upset, but reluctant to talk then and there and Lumley had no intention of pressing the matter. The note which had arrived in his pigeon-hole that afternoon had spoken of the lad's desperate need to talk to the chaplain—alone, in his rooms—and pleaded that no one else was to be told of this.

The chaplain had confirmed that this sort of thing

Lessons in Love

wasn't unusual, he'd encouraged all the young gentlemen to come to him if they needed a confidential talk, without fear of exposure or judgment. He'd never been called to see this particular chap before and knew very little of him except to note his regular attendance in chapel, as was hoped and expected of all college members.

The door had been open when Lumley reached the room at about ten o'clock, he'd known the time from having heard the chimes of St. Bride's bells. The window had been open, too—unusual on such a cold night, especially with Russell-Clarke in a state of some undress. The chaplain had become increasingly distressed at this point in the interview, retelling the shock of discovery, finding the bruises on the body and the spiteful little note.

Inspector Wilson had no wish to prolong the ordeal so had thanked him for his help, quietly asking Stewart to make sure that the man reached his rooms safely and wasn't left alone. As it turned out, alone is what the chaplain had wanted to be and he would brook no argument. "Thank you, Dr. Stewart, but I feel the need of quiet prayer and reading. I think I will contemplate all the times Our Lord spoke about forgiveness and try to feel it in my heart. But it will be difficult, very difficult."

Jonty knew all about how difficult forgiveness was. Lying in a cold bed listening to the early hours of Friday ring through, he wondered how the families of the two young men could ever forgive their killer. There were things in his own life that had proved impossible to forgive, no matter how often he repeated the words of the Paternoster in chapel or said his own personal prayers. It hadn't been easy at boarding school, being such a pretty, gentle boy among older, tougher lads with little in the way of morals or conscience. He'd put those times behind him long ago, but to be able to forgive the perpetrators? He wasn't ready for that—not yet, perhaps not ever.

Eventually he managed to drift into some sort of fitful slumber, only to be awakened, what seemed like mere seconds later, by a fierce knocking on the door. He tried to stuff his head under the pillow, but the thundering wouldn't go away. He threw back his covers and stomped out of his bedroom. There was about to be a third murder at St. Bride's and he was going to commit it. He unlocked the door and swung it open, asked whether *a man couldn't have five minutes bloody peace in his own bed* and was brought up short by the sight of Coppersmith, tousled and lacking sleep himself.

"I'm sorry, Orlando." Stewart was within his own little piece of the college and reverted naturally to Christian names. And naturally the sight of Coppersmith was enough to melt his heart. "Come in and let me get you some tea."

"No, *I'm* sorry, Jonty. I just wanted to make sure that you were up to date with all the news—Inspector Wilson and his faithful hound Cohen were here first thing." Coppersmith took a seat at the miniscule table in the tiny kitchen; fellows at St. Bride's weren't expected to have company to meals in their rooms, particularly breakfast. Stewart was only able to offer rolls and jam as refreshment, but they seemed acceptable to his guest.

"Our friends in the police must be as tired as we, Orlando. It was well gone midnight by the time I got Lumley away to his rooms."

"I doubt they'd slept at all. They'd already spent the whole day talking to that clot of a history student." He took a great splodge of strawberry jam and loaded his bread.

Jonty was fascinated to see that he didn't get a jot of it on him. In contrast, Stewart's nightshirt was already smeared with sticky red patches and would soon be a mass of crumbs. As much as he fancied this man, there were things about him that were infuriating, his degree of neatness for one. "And what *is* going on with the lad in question? False confession, I guess, although what could have motivated him, I don't know."

"Exhaustion through overwork is to be the official line, but I understand the man has a habit of doing it. Last year

Lessons in Love

he declared that he was involved in the burglaries here and was arrested, before it was made plain that he'd been taking tea with the Master when two of them occurred. Was sent home for convalescence then and will be so again now."

Jonty rolled his eyes and poured the tea. "Why hasn't he just been sent down, Orlando? That seems by far the best solution."

"Friends in high places, Dr. Stewart. A word in the right ear works wonders. Anyway, Inspector Wilson told me that he never really took the boy seriously, but there was always the chance that the lad was being extremely clever. You know the sort of thing—make an obviously false confession to someone else's crime and then confess to the one you really did. Who would believe you a second time?" Coppersmith looked tired and worried, more so than Jonty had ever seen him.

"And are they sure it wasn't just such a cunning scheme?"

"So they say. He was caught out by another impeccable alibi; he'd been sitting by the window of his room, a well lit window I might add, Jonty, all the evening. One of his fellow historians had been sitting opposite at his own window, nursing a toothache and a foul temper. He'd observed him regularly, not particularly liking the man and trying to wish his own pain upon him."

"No chance of our friend sneaking out?"

"Very little—wrong end of the college for one thing, so he would have had to be away a while to get to J7, kill Lord Morcar and return again. And the student with the sore face had their court in view, too, so no chance of anyone creeping through." He took a huge swig of tea—Jonty always wondered how the man could tolerate his drinks so hot—and continued. "Anyway, the police have finished with Lord Morcar's rooms, gone over them with the finest toothed comb the constabulary possessed, I should think. Dr. Peters wants me to help clear them this morning, for the parents to collect the boy's effects." He sighed. "And I've that supervision to give first. I fear it will be a long day, Jonty." He reached over and gently touched his friend's hand. "And such a shame for us, this business."

Stewart smiled at the touch. "Why us more than the others, Orlando? It affects us all here."

Coppersmith stroked the hand again. "It's as I said two nights since. We can't afford to expose ourselves to danger. And after last evening, that seems such a cruel thing."

There were no appropriate words for Stewart to use in reply, so they sat and finished their meal in silence, both full of regret for what had almost been and what might never be until this business was sorted. When Coppersmith rose to go, he gave Jonty's hand another squeeze and smiled wistfully. "Will I see you later?"

Stewart shrugged his shoulders. "I've work to do down in the library, Orlando and then there's a meeting over dinner with some of the chaps there."

Coppersmith looked startled, he'd forgotten the English fellows' regular fortnightly 'meeting'. He'd long teased Jonty that this meeting was little more than an excuse for them to sample the delights of another hostelry—the visit to The Bishop's Cope had made him aware of that—and they would be enjoying the company of his friend while he sat alone in the Senior Common Room.

"I'll see you tomorrow lunchtime, Orlando. Please don't tell me you've also forgotten our invitation out?" He didn't need to be told—his friend's face made it plain enough. "And you must wear something different, you can't be seen at a sporting do in such a sober tie."

Coppersmith looked down at his neckwear. He liked the somber colors and the staid pattern, he'd two others just like it. "I don't want to change my tie and anyway, we were only out at St. Thomas' yesterday." He suddenly paled. "Must we go again?"

"Absolute duty to honor all accepted invitations. You seemed keen enough when we were at high table there last night."

Lessons in Love

"That was before...this second murder."

Jonty wondered whether his friend had meant to say *before we kissed in the garden.* "Life has to go on, Dr. Coppersmith. I for one feel an absolute need to assert the joys of existence in the face of such calamity." Jonty saw the disapproval in his friend's face and grasped his hand. "You think me hard-hearted, I'm sure, but I've known my own sorrows and the only way to fight them is to live life as well as you can. Will you do this for me, Orlando?"

Coppersmith considered, then sighed again, acknowledging defeat. "I'll see you at twelve tomorrow, I take it?"

"Twelve it is, by the porters' lodge. And change that tie before you see the Master, it's covered in jam."

Coppersmith looked at the offending item. "It is not."

Jonty leaned forward and smeared his sticky fingers down it. "It is now..."

Once his friend had gone, Stewart decided that there was no point in returning to bed, however great the temptation might be. He washed, dressed and tidied his room, perfunctorily, of course, not having the same affection for neatness as Coppersmith had. A small voice at the back of his head kept nagging at him; he'd been meaning to have a word with Jackson about that note on the body and now seemed as good a time as any.

He decided not to enquire at the porters' lodge for the location of Jackson's room and instead began to saunter around The Old Court until he spied the name on the board by H stairway. His knock brought a swift reply. Jackson wasn't out at lectures, but struggling with an essay about worms.

"Dr. Stewart, I wasn't expecting you, sir. I'm afraid my rooms are rather untidy." He opened the door wider to display what he must have regarded as a terrible mess, although the place was a sight tidier now than Jonty's rooms had been when he'd *finished* clearing up.

"I've no wish to intrude, Mr. Jackson, it's just that with

the events of last night fresh in my mind, I wanted to clarify some things."

"Last night, sir?"

Stewart suddenly realized that the young man hadn't the slightest idea that there'd been a second murder. "I think we'd better sit down, Jackson." They sat on the rather ragged armchairs that faced the meager fire and Jonty carefully explained what the chaplain had found in the room in Middle Court on Thursday evening.

"I had no idea, Dr. Stewart," Jackson eventually said, once he'd taken in what he'd been told. "I had a terrible stomach ache last night and took to my bed early. That's why it's such a mess in here." He swept a hand over the ridiculously tidy room. "Trumper came and looked after me, boiled up lemonade and made me drink it. Tasted ghastly but it worked a treat."

Jonty smiled and tried to look encouraging. "Jackson, I know it's painful to discuss it, but on Monday night, was the window open when you entered Lord Morcar's room?"

The lad considered. "I'm not sure, sir. The door was slightly ajar, as I told the police, but I don't remember the window. There would have been a draught, wouldn't there and I don't remember being cold."

Jonty nodded. He certainly remembered being chilled the moment he entered that room, not just because of the presence of the corpse.

"And it would have been odd for him to be half dressed in a cold room—too fond of his creature comforts was Douglas." Jackson abruptly stopped, sniffed, then pulled himself together.

Jonty had been told that this student was excellent at remembering facts, but incapable of any original thought and had rather a slow brain. Stewart watched, fascinated, as the slow realization dawned and Jackson's mind caught up with the discussion. Every bit of his thinking seemed to be played out on his face. "Do you think that the culprit might have tried to escape by the window? In which case, was he lurking in another one of Morcar's rooms?" The lad became pale, no doubt thinking of perhaps being quite so close to a murderer.

"I really do doubt it, Jackson. He'd have looked a damn sight more obvious shinning down a drainpipe straight into The Old Court, once you'd raised the hue and cry, than he would have done just slinking into a corner somewhere and emerging later." Jonty rose to leave. "Don't fret over it."

"Was there anything else, Dr. Stewart?"

"No, thank you. I think that you've told me quite enough." Jonty bounced swiftly down the staircase and across to the porter's lodge. There, cadging pen and paper, he penned a swift note to the great and good of the local constabulary, persuaded Summerbee to go and deliver it and set off to do some proper work.

Coppersmith's attempts to get some mathematical knowledge to penetrate the ape-like skulls of his undergraduates had been slightly more successful than usual, perhaps because the students were beginning to find him easier to talk to, somehow less dauntingly remote. He hoped they had no idea about the thing in his life, namely kissing Jonty Stewart, which had wrought such changes in him. He hoped the Master wouldn't notice anything different when they met in Morcar's room to begin their cheerless task. The accumulated effects of a life, albeit only those lugged up from the ancestral home in Hampshire, seemed sparse and sad. They sorted and packed them with immense care.

At the very back of the bookcase, Peters unearthed a few plain tomes. Opening them to investigate, he swiftly shut them again and turned pale. "I don't think that these are in any way suitable for returning to Lord Morcar's next of kin."

Orlando took the little volumes and frowned. "If you wish, I'll dispose of them, Master."

"On the fire would be best, Dr. Coppersmith."
"I understand, sir."

But the books didn't reach the fire that morning nor afternoon. Orlando had work to be marked, lectures made up-to-date and thinking to be done. Not just consideration of his beloved calculus, but of events concerning his beloved college, too. Two murders now and Inspector Wilson hardly any further forward. Although they were keeping open minds, the police seemed sure that the culprit came from within St. Bride's and were involved in the laborious process of taking details of where every college member was for the crucial part of Monday night. Now they'd have to begin the process again with the particulars for Thursday, hundreds of statements that would need checking and comparing. Coppersmith didn't envy anyone that task, no matter how logical and pleasingly methodical it might prove.

And at the end of it would there be just one man who couldn't adequately account for his whereabouts on the two evenings? Orlando doubted it. There were plenty of conscientious students at St. Bride's who could well have been penning long (and in some cases incomprehensible) essays in their rooms about *The Iliad* or the death of Napoleon on both occasions. In which case how could they hope to proceed? An awful idea came into his mind; *lay yourself and Jonty out as bait and see what ensues.*

Coppersmith shuddered. Nothing in the world was as precious to him as his friend, not the most elegant piece of theoretical proof, no matter that it was marked with QED at the bottom. No trap could ever be worth risking Jonty. The truth would have to be allowed to emerge slowly from donkey work and character study. Frustrated, he turned again to the convoluted solutions for simple problems that his students had handed him and set to work on demolishing them.

Taking his seat later on in the Senior Common Room, Orlando turned to ask Dr. Stewart what he had thought of

Lessons in Love

the salmon at dinner. His mouth was open to speak when he remembered his friend's absence, an absence screaming out from the empty chair next to his. Coppersmith felt suddenly so very alone; lonelier than he'd ever been all the long years before Stewart had arrived at the college, lonelier than during the solitary years of his boyhood when friendships were not encouraged, he being in his parents' estimation so far above the run of the local children. And for the first time in his life, he felt a pang of jealousy because other people were spending time with *his* friend.

He was used to having Jonty at his side in the SCR and to having the man buzzing somewhere in the background throughout the other parts of his college existence. Orlando wondered how he could have ever sat there alone all those years, with no little imp blethering on inconsequentially in the chair next to his. *Always want to sit in the chair next to you* had become a bit of an anthem between them and Coppersmith truly felt the meaning of it tonight.

He thought about the morning, holding hands with Jonty over breakfast and how he'd been half worried that the electricity between them mightn't spark again and half frightened that it would. Orlando's life was changing at a rapid pace and he wasn't sure he could keep up with it.

Coppersmith returned early to his set of rooms, stoked the fire and settled down with the books Peters had given him. He began to snap their spines with a view to breaking them up and fuelling the flames but curiosity got the better of him. He flicked through the volumes but could see no illustrations, which made him even more keen to know why the Master had reacted in so marked a manner.

He began to read, odd passages from here and there, and soon began to regret that he'd ever started. They contained what seemed to him such awful things; graphic accounts of men with men, acts of a sexual and violent nature that made Orlando feel physically sick. Everything he'd shared with Jonty had been beautiful—had felt pure and wholesome—nothing had been as sordid as the things these books detailed.

It was at this point that he began to understand what motive might lie behind the murders. If these writings could evoke such strong feelings of revulsion in him, while he was attracted to another man, then what effect might knowing such acts were being committed in St. Bride's have upon an unbalanced or deeply prejudiced mind?

Coppersmith took up all the books, hurriedly ripped them apart and repeatedly fed the fire with the pieces, not ceasing until the last leaf had been turned into ashes.

Chapter Five

"I'd begun to think that I would never again get you alone, Orlando. If there's a knock on the door this afternoon I won't open it, not if it were the King himself to offer me a place on the Privy Council. *Edward, old man* I'd say and he'd reply *Yes Jonathan, old cock?* because he is really very down to earth, Orlando. Did you know that my father used to be taken to play with the royal family as a child and he always says that the Prince, as he was then, was such a caution and—what was I saying?" The fourth glass of Black Velvet on a stomach that had lunched on only a few savory biscuits had been a complete mistake. They'd been given large glasses, their hosts proving exceedingly generous. Stewart had reached a rare state of elation for a man who was notoriously good at holding his drink. He repeated, "Orlando, what was I saying?"

Coppersmith couldn't seem to remember upon what fascinating subject Jonty had been discoursing. "I think that you might have been being disrespectful to somebody but as, for a change, it wasn't *me* I shall let the matter go."

Just how they'd ever got themselves invited to a rowing club party was a great mystery, particularly to Coppersmith, who'd just tagged along after his friend as usual. The intense strain that they'd been under had been eased by the first glass of the black and bubbly, and life became rapidly rosier with every subsequent one. Orlando had only managed two and a half and that had been enough to make him almost incapable. Jonty had been forced to remove him from the gathering before he disgraced himself. There had been vague mutterings about *too smoky in here, feel the need of a good wash* and some fumbling at waistcoat buttons. Stewart had retained enough presence of mind to whisk him out the door and past the college fountain, which Coppersmith had eyed longingly.

"Could do with a good shower, Dr. Stewart," he'd mumbled at the time and had made an attempt to remove his jacket.

"Not here, you clown! In the middle of St. Thomas' and in the middle of winter."

Orlando had merely looked blearily at him for reply and they'd slithered through the streets back to the sanctuary of Jonty's rooms. There, the need for cleanliness seemed to overcome Coppersmith again. "Could do with that bath now, Jonty." While St. Bride's had been behind the times in many things, it had been positively forward thinking about bathrooms. And an endless supply of hot water.

Coppersmith removed his jacket and began an attempt on his waistcoat buttons. Tricky little buggers these proved, all of them seeming to be too big to pass back through the holes from whence they came. Stewart stood in silent amazement, a rapid wave of both realization and sobriety passing through his brain. *He's going to take off all his clothes, here, in my rooms, and take a soak. In my bath. Then he's going to sober up and find himself naked, in my bath, and I daren't even begin to guess what he's going to say or do then. I'm not sure I know what I'd do, except pray I could resist seducing him.*

Coppersmith had successfully removed his waistcoat and was trying to get the upper hand on his shirt buttons,

Lessons in Love

which were putting up a manly resistance. "Don't fancy a dip yourself, Jonty?"

If you were completely sober, most certainly. As it is... "No, thank you, Orlando. I'll just go and start the thing running. I'd better find you something to dry yourself on as well." He busied himself in the bathroom, concentrating madly on the mundane acts of ensuring the right water temperature, finding a decent sized towel.

"Don't like it too hot, Jonty." Coppersmith appeared in the doorway. He'd secured a surprisingly rapid victory over the rest of his clothes and was both naked and brazen. Stewart concentrated very hard on keeping his gaze above waist level, which was distraction enough as Orlando had such a lovely, smooth chest, just soft enough to make a luxurious pillow. He wondered how it would feel to spend a night nestling on it.

"Then sort it out yourself. I'll go and make us a pot of tea, I have a feeling you'll need it in a minute." The refuge of the English in all moments of stress—*I'll put the kettle on, we'll have a nice cup of tea.* Jonty had laughed often enough when his female relatives had resorted to it, but now the caddy and the teapot provided a wonderful retreat from temptation.

Someone began to murder elephants in the bathroom. *Oh hell. Oh spite. He's started to sing and my misery is now complete.* Eventually the wholesale slaughter (not just of elephants, but of Gilbert and Sullivan, too) came to an end. Stewart heard gurgling water and wet footsteps and an extremely sheepish young man, clad only in towels, slunk into the kitchen. "Seem to have disgraced myself, Jonty."

Stewart sniggered. No matter how alluring a sight he was in those towels, Orlando embarrassed was always amusing. "Not half as much as you would have done if I hadn't dissuaded you from bathing in the fountain at St. Thomas'."

"I never tried to do that!" Coppersmith looked horrified. "Did I?"

55

"You seemed very eager an hour ago, but luckily your friend Jonty can hold his drink."

"What else have I done? I seem to be in a state of undress, but I can't remember anything since drinking that second black velvet."

"You've done nothing Orlando, honestly, other than strip naked and utilize my bath." Stewart smiled indulgently at Coppersmith's increasing discomfort and pushed a hot cup of tea across the table. "Strong, with plenty of sugar. I think you need the pick-me-up."

Orlando looked back through the doorway into the main room, saw his discarded clothing and blanched. "Did I ... parade around?"

Jonty felt torn between the delight he took in his friend's discomfort and the concern that the man's distress caused him; concern won the day. "No, never worry, you were really quite discreet." He hastily put away the recollection of Coppersmith standing in the bathroom doorway being anything but prudent. The man had such an attractive body, there had been such beauty in its brief moment of shamelessness.

"Should get dressed, I suppose."

"Have your tea first, I've got some Chelsea buns somewhere." Stewart reached for a tin and extracted two reasonably fresh ones. "Didn't get a proper breakfast today and very little since. Think we should both eat." Which they did, in silence. The buns provided not only nourishment but an excuse not to have to talk, to simply gather thoughts and regroup. Stewart was fairly certain that they were on the verge of something momentous here, if he could keep Coppersmith focused and calm. They hadn't touched in any significant way since the night in the Fellows' Garden; Orlando had made sure since then that they'd barely had the chance to even be alone. Jonty understood his motivation, his fears, but he was still deeply frustrated. He reached a sticky, currant covered hand over the table and grasped an equally sugary one of Coppersmith's.

Lessons in Love

"It's just me here with you, Orlando. Nothing you can do will embarrass or upset me. *Always want to sit in the chair next to yours*, remember?"

Coppersmith managed a smile, but the extreme discomfort he must have been feeling was plain. He shivered. "Feeling a bit cold sitting *here*, Jonty."

"Well let's get you next to the fire then. Go and stir some life into the thing while I wrestle another cup out of the pot."

After a minute or two, Jonty backed into the room bearing a tray with the drinks and some shortbread he'd discovered. Orlando had coaxed the fire into a cheerful blaze and had then dropped onto the mat before it, looking rosy and content in the glow. They ate and drank again in companionable silence, Stewart reflecting all the while that his aunts had probably been absolutely right to swear by the civilizing and restorative effects of afternoon tea. Being before the fire together felt absolutely blissful.

Orlando broke the tranquility. "I feel a bit of an idiot sitting here in a towel, with you fully dressed, Jonty. Should be getting dressed myself, I suppose." Despite what he said, he didn't show the slightest inclination to take his own advice.

"There is another solution, of course," Jonty ventured. "For your embarrassment; another way to solve the problem. Bear with me for just a moment." He rose and went into the bathroom, feeling a bit of an idiot as well. This was either going to be a masterstroke or a complete disaster. He found himself a large towel and began to undress.

He hadn't dared do this in front of Coppersmith, it would have given the man too much time to become skittish and object. Anyway, the act of disrobing was never an elegant one. The top half was fine, very alluring it had been to watch Orlando stripping off his jacket and waistcoat, but the bottom half presented all sorts of logistical difficulties. There was the significant risk of hopping around with one leg still in your trousers, which presented a very unappetizing sight, or worse still being left in just your socks, which was a complete passion killer. Better to present yourself in the best possible light, he mused, removing the last item, the offending socks, and draping the towel around himself. He took a very deep breath and went back into the main room.

"Now we're equal." Jonty took his place next to his friend in front of the hearth.

Orlando's jaw had dropped when he saw Stewart entering the room. Jonty could imagine him struggling to regain his composure but failing. "Jonty, you absolute oaf!" Coppersmith started to laugh, which was a rare enough occurrence at any time and one that always set Stewart off giggling as well. They didn't stop until the tears were streaming down their faces.

"Oh, Orlando—your face. I've not seen you so shocked since that lady from Girton invited you to step outside with her and admire the wallflowers."

Coppersmith blushed at the remembrance. Stewart knew that he really did hate talking to women and this one had been rather too persistent. Orlando looked across at his friend and noticed the small, exquisite gold crucifix around his neck. "May I?" he reached over and began to finger it gently. "This is a lovely piece of workmanship. Do you wear it often?"

"Always." Stewart smiled wistfully. "My grandmother bought it for me when I came up to Bride's as a student. I've worn it every day that I've been at the college, now and before."

Coppersmith kept rubbing the delicate gold chain until his fingers must have grown numb and sought for softer contact. Letting the necklace go, he tentatively traced the line of Jonty's collarbone. "This is a lovely piece of workmanship, too. And this," his hand worked its way down his friend's chest, toying with the hairs that were sparsely scattered along the way.

Lessons in Love

"Orlando," Stewart whispered hoarsely, "you don't need to do this."

Coppersmith swiftly removed his hand, as if confused that Stewart didn't seem to want his touches. "I'm sorry, Jonty, I...I hoped that you would like me to do it."

"Well, of course I would, you clot, but I don't want you to feel under any duress. Not after all that we said yesterday about exposing ourselves to danger." He gently took Coppersmith's hand and returned it to his chest, placing it over his heart. "Beating for you, Orlando, just for you, and it can wait until this business is done." His face melted into one of its golden smiles which only stopped when Coppersmith leaned over and kissed him, not just the once, but several times, each one longer and more intense than the one before. He'd never been so passionate before and Jonty found it exhilarating. Their towels were loosened in the scrimmage of arms and bodies until Coppersmith broke their contact, gasping like a swimmer coming up for air. He laid his head on Stewart's chest, relaxing and regaining his composure. "I've been reading a book, Jonty."

Stewart giggled again. "Orlando, I don't know who coaches you in romantic conversation, but they're leading you badly astray. It would be far more apt at a moment like this to say *Shall I compare thee to a summer's day?*" He stroked Coppersmith's head gently; he'd dreamed of this moment, or one like it, often and the fact that too much alcohol had made his body incapable of responding as it naturally should was probably just as well, given the other man's lack of experience.

Coppersmith thumped Stewart's chest, temporarily knocking all the breath and sauce out of his friend. "I'm being serious. You know that Dr. Peters asked me to help him prepare Lord Morcar's effects for his family. Given the delicate nature of this business he couldn't leave it to anyone else, which was just as well, as we found some books hidden away. They would have caused his family even more distress if they'd known of their existence, and I offered to destroy the things. I was unwise enough to read parts of them first."

A great shivering sigh passed through Orlando's body. Jonty could guess what those books might contain and why they'd distressed his friend so much. He held the man closer, so that he'd be warmed not just by the fire but by the warmth of their affection. "Did they upset you greatly, Orlando?"

Coppersmith faintly nodded his head. "Such scandalous, disgusting things they talked about, Jonty, things that I couldn't imagine us doing." He seemed sickened at the memory of what he had seen in their pages.

Stewart remained quiet, speechless with both awe at such prodigious ingenuousness and concern for the fright Orlando had taken. At last he'd realized that Coppersmith's innocence was a rare, shining, precious thing, not to be ridden over roughshod for his or anyone else's desires. All thought of initiating his friend there and then in the ultimate delights of the flesh evaporated like mist on a spring day. It could wait, it would have to wait, it was too valuable a commodity to waste imprudently and risk losing him.

"Think we should be getting dressed, Orlando," he ventured at last, but his only reply were regular, calm breaths. Coppersmith had fallen asleep, mentally and physically exhausted, like a babe at his mother's breast, and he stayed sleeping until Jonty had to wake him to get dressed for Hall.

"Is that a wraith or is it you, Orlando? I do believe you have a hangover!" Jonty Stewart stood at the door grinning madly and bearing a small paper bag.

"If that's the correct term for an entire team of coal miners working a new seam in my head, then I have, Jonty. I have indeed." The wraith beckoned him into the room and then slumped on the sofa.

"I've brought you bulls-eyes," Stewart waggled the

sweets. "I saw you'd missed chapel and suspected you needed a bit of bucking up."

"Bucking up? I think I'm going to die. Just don't let them play 'Abide With Me' at my funeral. I want 'Jerusalem' and 'Cwm Rhondda'." Coppersmith shut his eyes and groaned.

The last few hours had been agony, his head thumping, his stomach churning and his brain entirely confused at the events of the day before. Memories of black velvet, cold and delicious, mingled with memories of fingering Jonty's crucifix, the metal feeling cool and smooth and as pleasing to the touch as the skin that lay beneath it. He'd never had the privilege of being in such close contact with Jonty before and it had felt wonderful. He remembered feeling elated and bold, then being upset at the memories of Morcar's books and finally desperately tired and rather uncertain about what had been going on between him and Jonty.

"You won't die as long as I can get enough coffee into you." Stewart made straight for the kitchen, putting on the kettle then re-entering the main room to twitch the curtains open slightly.

"Jonty! You've already tried to deafen me with that racket in the kitchen, must you blind me as well?" Coppersmith guessed he looked even more spectral in the pale January light.

"Brought you some bulls-eyes, but if you're going to be an ungrateful wretch, I shall eat them all. Slowly. While you're watching." Stewart picked one out from the paper bag. "This looks particularly tempting," and popped it in his mouth.

"I don't think I'd even care if you ate the entire contents of the sweet shop."

Stewart looked shocked. "You must be feeling especially ropy to make such a remark." It had long been a joke between them that Coppersmith had one solitary, little vice and that was eating sweeties. They'd been strolling down King's Parade one afternoon when Orlando had suddenly grabbed Stewart's arm and dragged him into a small alley. Glancing furtively around, he'd then dragged them into a dimly lit confectionery shop where the proprietor knew him well enough to address Coppersmith by name. He was a regular and valued customer, a habitual purchaser of Liquorice Allsorts, toffees and other delights and it was the one place in Cambridge outside the University that he'd visited with pleasure in the days before he met Jonty.

Discovering this little secret had thrilled Stewart and he'd make a point of leaving little bags of boiled sweets or boxes of Mint Lumps in Coppersmith's pigeon hole. For a while, Orlando had thought that he'd acquired a secret female admirer who'd somehow bribed the porters into placing these love tokens among his mail. It was only when Stewart, bursting with curiosity as to why his friend never referred to these offerings, had asked him outright, "Did you enjoy the bulls-eyes, Dr. Coppersmith?" that he'd realized what was going on. And he'd been ridiculously delighted that the sender was his own Jonty and not some desperate harridan from Girton.

Orlando felt beyond even the reach of Liquorice Allsorts this particular Sunday morning. He sipped apathetically at the coffee Jonty gave him, rejected a slice of toast and refused to have *the hair of the dog*. "It was *the hair of the dog* you suggested last night at table. *A glass of white wine will see you right as rain, Dr. Coppersmith.* Well, look at me now and examine your conscience, Dr. Stewart." For the first time in their acquaintance he felt really irate with Jonty and he was going to let the man know about it.

"I'll examine it all you want, but I doubt my conscience will prick me, it's as clear as a newborn child's. As for your hangover, I've a bit of a thumping head myself, but *I'm* not making such a song and dance about it as *some people* are. Men who can't handle their Black Velvet should stick to

Lessons in Love

lemonade." Jonty snorted, causing Coppersmith to shudder. "I suppose the only way to make you feel better is to get you to think. Well, I had an interesting talk with Jackson on Friday."

Stewart related the conversation in detail and Orlando experienced the odd sensation of feeling appreciably better with every fact told to him and every detail which he could catalogue and consider. As soon as they reached the point about the window being shut, Coppersmith seized on it, grasping the essential point that Jackson had missed. "The murderer must have returned to the room and seen the note missing, most likely. But why should he, just to open a window?"

Stewart shrugged. "Why do any of it, Orlando? Why take a life? Why leave such a vindictive message? We seem to be dealing with insanity, here. Perhaps there's no use in applying logic."

"I wonder what Russell-Clarke wanted to talk to the chaplain about?" Coppersmith reached for the bag of bulls-eyes, took one and looked at it carefully. *Perhaps I'm regaining the will to live.*

"I would imagine that he was frightened, as you were for us. I dare say that our friends Mr. Wilson and Mr. Cohen will soon find that the lad shared Lord Morcar's inclinations. Perhaps he thought that making a clean breast of it to the chaplain would somehow help. He might even have feared for his own life and wanted to face death shriven." Stewart shivered at the thought.

Orlando offered his friend a bulls-eye and took another for himself. He explained his own ideas of the afternoon before; the hope that eliminating all those with alibis would leave one person, or at least a very small group of suspects.

Jonty seemed to consider. "I think you're being too optimistic, Orlando. I expect that a whole string of students will happen to have no one to vouch for them at the two times in question. Fellows of the college just the same. And they will all probably turn out to be innocent, as a guilty man would no doubt seek to cover his tracks and ensure a series of impeccable alibis." He pondered again. "How far do you think we should get involved in this, Orlando? You were asked to keep your eyes and ears open and that we've done. Should we be taking more direct action?"

The thought of making themselves bait passed through Coppersmith's mind again but he quickly dismissed it. "What did you have in mind?"

"Going out and asking around, like I did with Jackson. Indulging in the very sort of gossip that Dr. Peters told us not to. I find it highly likely that someone would tell us things that they might not want to reveal to the police, or would think too trivial to mention." He stopped, smiling. "That's it, have another bulls-eye, Orlando, we'll have you back to your usual self soon. Anyway, I don't think that anyone can solve this by simply sitting in a darkened room and thinking."

Coppersmith felt distinctly thwarted. He'd rather begun to fancy the thought of sitting in a room and unraveling the mystery. To have to go and actually talk to people wasn't so appealing an idea. "And do you think that we should do this, Jonty?"

"Yes, I do. We need to go out and play our part in finding this madman. But not until you look less like a drunken tramp." He came over and kissed Coppersmith on the brow. "Tidy yourself up and I'll take you out for lunch. Then we can come back here and make a plan of campaign, after I've kissed you properly at least half a dozen times, that is."

Orlando now felt as if he'd definitely found the reason to live again. Whether it was the pleasing thought of lunch or the exciting one of the half dozen kisses, he couldn't tell, but he went off to find his razor and a clean shirt, feeling content. Even though he was leaving Stewart in possession of the last bulls-eye and a self-satisfied smile.

Chapter Six

Inspector Wilson appeared in college again on the Sunday afternoon. He lacked his usual companion, who'd been struck down with a cold and was presently lying in his bed at home, sneezing. He called on Dr. Peters, who turned out to be taking tea with the Vice-Chancellor, so made his way over to Dr. Coppersmith's set of rooms.

He knocked on the door, was welcomed in by both Coppersmith and Stewart, then ushered to a seat in front of a roaring fire, Orlando dragging another chair over so that all three of them could take some warmth. Stewart disappeared into the kitchen in search of his beloved tea caddy and some pink-iced buns that had so far survived the two fellow's depredations.

They'd both already consumed an excellent lunch at The Bishop's Cope, Coppersmith having declared that he could feel quite at home in that particular public house, and were at present 'planning their campaign', having indulged in the necessary number of kisses, with one or two 'for luck' as Jonty put it. Over their steaming cups of tea, they compared notes with the constabulary.

Wilson reported that Sergeant Cohen had been to

interview *those boys who could be found in certain parts of the city should you need* as he coyly referred to them. They'd found one or two who'd had dealings with Lord Morcar, but they could unearth no new information. "As far as we can tell, these boys know nothing of Russell-Clarke; I assume that the young man didn't pay for his pleasures, or at least didn't purchase them there. And I must thank you, Dr. Stewart, for your note. We should have been sharp enough to pick up the matter of the window ourselves."

Jonty seemed slightly embarrassed, and muttered that he'd only kept the window in mind as he'd suffered so much from the roaring gale coming through it. The three of them debated a reason that the murderer might have had for returning, but the conversation proved sterile.

"In any case, I'm glad that I asked for your assistance." Wilson bore what seemed to be a genuinely friendly, avuncular smile. "My superior officers weren't convinced that it was the best of tactics, and I'm glad that it's bearing fruit. Now, you'll want to know about alibis…"

There was little to report, the business of checking them still being underway, and eventually Orlando decided that he and Stewart should come clean about their plans. "We were thinking that we might talk to some of the students, very informally, to see whether we could get them to tell us anything that they might be unwilling to divulge to you."

"It's a serious business, withholding evidence from the police, Dr. Coppersmith," Wilson remarked, not without a smile. "But it happens often enough, particularly if people get a bit twitchy about the truth, like that young clot Jackson. They act from the best of motives, but it never helps. Just as well that his friend made him see a bit of sense."

"Do you think that we'll achieve anything in doing this, Inspector? We seem to have been of little use so far." Jonty was no doubt trying not to appear to be treading on the constabulary's toes.

"I don't think that you can do any harm, Dr. Stewart,

Lessons in Love

except if you put yourselves directly at risk."

Coppersmith froze, convinced that the Inspector had discovered their relationship; his thoughts ran to the dock and two years' hard labor.

"I mean, of course, the risk that you might appear to the murderer to be too interested in his doings. He may not confine his violence to his targeted victims." Wilson shook his head as if he'd seen such things before.

Coppersmith let out a sigh of relief, which proved so loud that he was thankful when Jonty quickly covered it with a question. "All the students would know me as a terrible gossip. My friend here will tell you that I rarely stop chatting. I'd hope that my questions would be interpreted as natural loquaciousness."

Wilson nodded. "That seems reasonable, as long as your curiosity is not out of place. I don't want another corpse or two to deal with." He rose. "I'd be grateful if you let the Master know what I've told you, gentlemen, and please let us know what you find, as soon as you find it. I remind you again to take care." The Inspector shook their hands, donned his hat and left.

"Thought we'd been caught out there, all that stuff about putting ourselves at risk." Coppersmith reached for the last cake, then changed his mind. "Jonty, I have something to ask of you." Orlando hesitated. Something was troubling him and he didn't know how to express it.

Stewart raised an eyebrow. "Ask away, Orlando, although if it's a request to borrow my copies of Conan Doyle so that you can swot up on your detective techniques, I may well refuse. You'll get them covered in jam, like your tie was."

"Jonty, I am trying to be serious." Coppersmith frowned; it cost him so much to bare his emotions and he hated to be made game of when he was making such an effort.

"You're always trying to be serious, Orlando, it is one of your most endearing qualities." Stewart gently took his friend's hand and pressed it tenderly. The gesture spoke more than any amount of words would.

"A few days ago I suggested that we should only remain friends while this killer remains uncaught. I can't support that suggestion any longer, not after the last few days." Coppersmith's frown changed to a pleading look; he wanted to make amends somehow for all the daft things he'd said but couldn't see how to proceed.

"Orlando, I'm glad you've come to that conclusion. We can't live our lives in the shadow of fear. I know, I've lived in dread and terror myself and it doesn't do anyone any good. Keep your door locked, don't walk alone at night, but don't stop kissing me. Especially after yesterday." They sealed the bargain with a kiss, parted until hall and Coppersmith was left musing how it would be impossible to ever give up being so close to this wonderful man.

Dr. Coppersmith didn't eat much at high table that Sunday night, having indulged so mightily at lunch, but Jonty held no such inhibitions, tucking in as if he hadn't seen a square meal for months. Orlando was amazed at the quantity of food that was being shoveled down Stewart's gullet, until he remembered the sights of the afternoon before, when he'd been blessed with a glimpse, quite a substantial and delightful glimpse, of his friend's physique. *Muscles in his spit* was an expression he'd heard Jonty use regarding an opposition forward in a rugby game and it would have been an apt one for Stewart himself. It had proved a complete contrast to Orlando's own slim frame and he couldn't help thinking about that brawny chest all the way through Hall.

The two men took coffee in the Senior Common Room, happy in their usual chairs. The other fellows were delighted to see that whatever they'd argued about on Wednesday seemed to have been resolved, which was a great relief to all, as a bad-tempered Coppersmith was more

Lessons in Love

than anyone could have borne. Jonty and Orlando discussed St. Bride's rugby team's chances in the cup and they mused upon the likelihood of Lee being made Head Porter when the present incumbent retired. They talked about anything that wasn't murder, or romance. Now they would take more than usual care in public to appear to be only friends.

Jonty embarked on a long speech and wasn't happy that Coppersmith appeared to be ignoring him. He wondered if the man's mind had been dwelling in pleasant memories of the two of them in front of the fire, so simply tapped his arm gently to bring him back to the present.

"I beg your pardon, Dr. Stewart, I was lost in my thoughts. Please repeat what you were saying."

"I simply asked whether you'd ever been in a punt before, because I have a distinct desire to become reacquainted with one. Soon."

"A punt?" Coppersmith's eyebrows looked like they were going to disappear around the back of his head. "In the last week of January. A punt. You'll never be able to hire one for a start." He snorted and sat back, as if the argument were already won and Jonty would never be able to overcome his logic.

"Don't need to hire one, there's a splendid one down at The White Hart which the landlord will let us use on Wednesday, should we wish. Asked him on Friday night. And I know that you're free that afternoon, as the dunderheads will be chasing some variety of ball around a pitch"

"You have a worrying familiar acquaintance with the local hostelries, Stewart. Anyway, we can't go this week, the weather's still bloody freezing."

Jonty noted the swear word and reveled in the influence he was having on his strait-laced friend. *He wouldn't have said that word two months ago. If only I could get him to loosen up on other fronts.* He sighed and continued the assault. "Then wear your hat and scarf and gloves, because I have the urge to take you down to Grantchester and go you will."

Orlando seemed reluctant to admit defeat even in the face of such determination. "Can't it wait until the summer?" A cunning little thought must have occurred to him. "In July we could easily find a nice drooping willow, moor underneath it out of view and enjoy a bottle of bubbly. Enjoy all sorts of things."

His intended victim wasn't taken in. "You wouldn't even dare a peck on the cheek in public, in broad daylight, behind a screen of willow branches or not, so don't try to tempt me with promises of romantic delight." Jonty considered for a moment. "Actually it'll be a lot quieter on the river in January than in July and we won't even need the cover of the trees." He produced a rather lascivious smirk. "This trip becomes more and more appealing, Dr. Coppersmith."

Orlando was defeated. "I guess I'll have to fish out my long johns if I can't avoid a trip equivalent to setting out for the North Pole." He rolled his eyes as if to say that this Wednesday was going to be a particularly trying one.

Before Wednesday came there were Monday and Tuesday to be negotiated. No further acts of violence sullied the college, but the news from the police wasn't encouraging. Of the two hundred or so students in residence, thirty had been on their own on both occasions and many more had been without an alibi for one or the other. Even one of the fellows couldn't be eliminated from enquires on this basis, although the fact that the man could barely climb the two stairs up to the SCR without aid had made him a highly unlikely assailant of healthy young men.

Stewart had decided to start his enquiries properly and so the process began at the Monday afternoon's English tutorial. The combined intellects of the students had been stretched by the consideration of *King Lear*, with Trumper making some excellent observations about the possible

Lessons in Love

interpretations of some of the lines. Stewart took off his spectacles, which was a signal that the official business of the supervision had finished. He dispensed toffees all round and innocently remarked, "Well, I suppose that you young louts have the whole mystery sorted out and are only withholding the solution from the police because you want to see them squirm."

A young lad called MacKenzie grinned. "Wish we did, sir. It would make life a lot easier. Perhaps then the porters would stop treating this place like some sort of a prison. Ingleby here has a theory that the culprit is a woman who's entered the college masquerading as a man and is wreaking vengeance on the male sex."

"That's not what I said," Ingleby protested, "I only remarked that it wouldn't surprise me if it *were a woman*. My actual theory is that someone has an unrequited crush on one of the fellows and is murdering people out of sheer sexual frustration!"

Trumper blushed at this remark. Jonty noticed and felt sorry for the lad—he suspected that Trumper had a bit of a 'thing' for his English tutor. Luckily the blush went unnoticed in the general uproar that greeted Ingleby's use of the phrase 'sexual frustration', young MacGrath being horrified that such a disgraceful thing should be mentioned. Jonty wondered how they would ever cope when they got around to analyzing *Othello*.

"Oh, you do talk rot," sniffed Mackenzie, "sexual frustration my elbow. It's obvious that these crimes have been committed by someone who absolutely abhors sexual relations. Look for someone very righteous and full of preaching. How about the chaplain?"

There was another uproar of protest. *No one should suspect the chaplain, he's never preachy at all, full of love they neighbor*. And, as Jonty knew but kept to himself, the man was the possessor of two immaculate alibis, which was more than could be said for the four young men in the room. MacGrath was in the clear, having been in the sickbay for the best part of the last two weeks, quarantined because of an attack of mumps. His visitors had been few and far between, given the risks associated with the disease, but the college nurse had vouched for him without hesitation and no one would have been man enough to argue with her. The other three could account for only one evening between them, when Trumper had been with his pal Jackson, ministering to the man's stomach disorder on the Thursday. Otherwise they had each been on their own, working, or so they said. Stewart had seen the results of this alleged devotion to learning and it wouldn't have even impressed Dr. Coppersmith, let alone an expert on Shakespeare's tragedies.

Jonty tried again. "So who do you know who fits your description, Mackenzie? I can think of a few people from when I studied here who would have proved a perfect match, but now..."

Ingleby rose to the bait. "There's someone living in The Middle Court, don't know his name, but I think he's reading Law. I've heard him sounding off to people more than once about *the lack of morals in modern society*. He thinks Lumley is far too forgiving and unwilling to take people to task for their sins. Said that he *would know how to deal with some of the scoundrels that infest the college*."

Dr. Stewart rolled his eyes. "Strikes me that a Christian's duty *is* to forgive and not to judge and I seem to think that there were some fairly clear instructions given along those lines." He waited while his reference to scripture penetrated the skulls of his listeners. "And have you told all this to the police, Ingleby?"

"Oh no, sir. Just in case he turns out to have nothing to do with it."

"When will you young idiots learn that the truth must be told where murder is concerned? Write down what you've told me and I'll get the porters to deliver it." He looked around the small group, fixing them with a very sharp glare. "None of the rest of you have any little

Lessons in Love

revelations that you'd like to make?"

There was a shaking of heads all round and a few distinctly wary looks. Dr. Stewart decided that he'd little further to gain at this point from these young men and ushered them out, once Ingleby had committed his information to paper. Jonty had no concrete source on which to base his supposition, but he'd a nagging feeling that these lads still had more to tell and he was jiggered if he knew how to extract it from them.

Dr. Coppersmith had tried to perform a similar act of information gathering from his Tuesday students. Lacking Jonty's natural charm and ease, he'd not the slightest idea how to tackle the subject and launched into an incoherent diatribe about recent events, the honor of the college, the value of honesty and his willingness to lend a sympathetic ear. His listeners had just about grasped his earlier thoughts on differential calculus but this last speech had been beyond them.

"Please, Dr. Coppersmith," ventured Ferguson, a Highland Scot and by far the bravest of the young men present, "could you say that again, because we didn't grasp your meaning."

Orlando couldn't say it again, as he'd confused himself. "I just wondered if any of you knew anything about these murders."

There was a dawning of understanding in the room. "Oh, that!" remarked Valentine, who was an old Etonian and best friend of Ferguson, despite their being geographically and socially disparate. Coppersmith had never understood their friendship, not until Dr. Stewart had come along. "Word among the tables at Hall is that one of the first year students, I think he's from Harrow or somewhere equally disreputable, is affected by the full moon and thinks he's a werewolf. Goes out looking for blood."

Coppersmith looked intently at the young lad and frowned. "If that's all you have to say for yourself, Valentine, then you can shut up. I may not be an astronomer, but even I can recognize that the moon is only waxing now, and I'm not a dolt to be made game of so."

The young lad blushed and the other students looked anywhere but at him or their tutor. They'd all attempted in the past to get one over on this intellectually rigorous but eminently gullible fellow and very successful they'd been at it, Orlando not noticing when he was being ridiculed. But the man was becoming a little too worldly wise to succumb to their teasing now.

"I have something to say," the deep highland tones of Ferguson broke the embarrassed silence. "Someone goes about spying in this college. There are nights I can't sleep. It's far too hot down in this part of the world." (Coppersmith remembered the freezing nights they had recently endured and inwardly marveled.) "I sit and look at the stars, or go out into The Middle Court and observe them through my telescope. A number of times I've seen a figure furtively darting in and out of stairwells, creeping about. One night I followed him for a wee while and I was sure he was listening at doors."

"And you thought not to tell Inspector Wilson?"

"My family have seen fit not to offer information voluntarily to the authorities for many a generation. I will not begin now," and Ferguson set his face in such a hard expression that Coppersmith himself would have struggled to imitate it. He supposed he'd have to bite the bullet and tell Inspector Wilson himself.

Tuesday night after high table, the glow of firelight illuminated two relaxed figures in Stewart's rooms. They'd compared what they'd learned from their students, information which they'd shared with the police. The identity of the law student with the large mouth had been

Lessons in Love

easily established and he was at present entertaining Inspector Wilson with accounts of what he'd said and why. The boy's name was Marchbanks and he was in the category of those who had an alibi for both murders, so the police had little hope of this being the killer, but the alibis were being scrutinized very carefully a second time. They hadn't so far identified Ferguson's 'spy'.

The two fellows of St. Bride's at least had the agreeable feeling that they were doing something positive to try to lift the cloud hanging over their college but they were frustrated that a solution seemed to be taking so long to appear. They shared a glass of port and watched the fire with as much contentment as they could muster.

Coppersmith put the glass down and drew Stewart to him for a kiss or three. Orlando had become quite an accomplished kisser, a quick learner as Jonty had always surmised, and didn't restrict himself to his friend's lips, but was brave enough now to pepper his friend's face with kisses and extend the honor to his ears and neck. For Stewart this was delightful, despite the fact that he still yearned for more. He knew that he should be grateful for any physical display from this reserved and self-conscious young man and recognized that he was more fortunate than his poor sister had been. She'd shared barely more than the tiniest of kisses with her fiancé before their marriage and her wedding night had been a great shock to her, occasioning her return, in tears, to their mother the next morning.

But Saturday had opened up such incredible possibilities, even though Jonty suspected that Orlando had been aided in his ardor and daring by the Black Velvet. That was evident by the fact that he still didn't seem to know what to do with his hands while they were kissing, usually just moving them clumsily through his friend's hair or over his back. Jonty, while systematically consuming his lover's left ear, decided to risk sticking his hand up the back of Coppersmith's shirt. The immediate tension this caused in

Orlando made him stop.

"Just checking whether your vest will be thick enough for going out in that punt tomorrow, Orlando." Jonty recognized that he'd overstepped the mark and resorted, as ever, to humor. "Think this style is a little too flimsy, have you anything woollier?"

"Only your brain," Coppersmith essayed, in obvious discomfort. Jonty wondered if the thought of *those* books still nagged at him, but thought better of asking. Orlando gave Stewart a last, long kiss and rose to go. "The White Hart at one o'clock?"

"Aye aye, sir." Jonty gave a mock naval salute, in honor of their proposed taking to the water. "I'll come straight down from the library." He opened the door and watched his friend go down the stairs, sad that they couldn't seem to progress beyond this point. He'd become excited in Orlando's arms, much more excited than he'd been when they'd wrestled the previous Saturday, when over-indulgence in alcohol had rendered all his physical responses sluggish. And now he was left alone, again; aroused. Stewart desperately hoped that Orlando's skittishness was due only to those wretched books. He could guess at their salacious nature and imagined that the acts they described might be savage and bestial. If this were the case, Coppersmith could be slowly won round by educating him that love could be gentle and kind, that the physical side could complement and fulfill the spiritual.

His dread was that the problem lay deeper than that. Perhaps Orlando simply couldn't indulge in anything more than kissing and caressing. Jonty had known a chap at University College who'd been self-confessedly ascetic, not wishing to take part in any romantic activity with another person. Like Coppersmith, this man had been fastidious, almost obsessively tidy. The thought of the essential messiness of even a deep kiss had horrified him and the idea of another pair of hands (hands that were possibly less than immaculately clean) touching him had been appalling. If

Orlando, sober and in control, felt like this, then there was very little hope.

Jonty realized that he had been standing looking at the stairway for a long time. *Cold shower and a cup of tea, Dr. Stewart*, he told himself, closing and carefully locking the door.

Chapter Seven

"You never cease to amaze me, Coppersmith—you've been here six years and not set foot in *The Bishop's Cope*. Now you tell me that you've never been in one of these!" They'd left *The White Hart* behind them and Stewart had soon got the knack again of propelling this strange craft. "You'd better be watching closely, my friend, because when we reach that old oak tree over there, you're going to be doing the punting."

Orlando couldn't have felt more sullen if he tried. It was no good arguing with Jonty, because the obstinate little swine would always have the last word. He would just have to take his punishment like a man. They moored, they swapped places, then Stewart lay back on the blanket he'd lugged all the way from St. Bride's and looked self-satisfied.

"Well, get on with it, man."

Coppersmith sniffed. "I'm merely considering this procedure logically." Jonty snorted, but his friend carried on in a dignified manner. He slowly drew the pole up and began to act in as close an imitation of Stewart as he could manage. In spite of his sulking, he had in fact been taking a keen, if surreptitious, interest in the technique employed in propelling the punt. He was determined to show the other man what he could do if he applied himself. They moved off from the bank successfully enough but then they began to turn in circles.

"Dr. Coppersmith, I think you're probably dropping the pole too far away from the craft. Try to put it closer." He tried, it worked, and they moved along the river.

Soon Orlando had the thing mastered and became quite blasé. He bet that Jonty was concerned that he'd overreach himself and lose the pole, so was dogged in his determination not to do so. Although the day was cold, it was bright and the journey was a very pleasant one, as long as you could bear the risk of essential parts of your anatomy dropping off. They left behind the problems of the college and the temptations of playing at Sherlock Holmes and they glided smoothly on.

Coppersmith now felt possessive over the punt pole, resisting all Jonty's suggestions that *he* might be allowed another go; Orlando was proud of his newly acquired skill and he wanted to show it off. In the end, Stewart had to threaten to capsize the craft to get his friend to stop. They pulled into the bank and found not a soul in sight, unless you counted three particularly stupid looking cows in the adjacent field. Coppersmith sat down and rubbed his hands, which were beginning to get sore, despite his thick leather gloves.

Jonty looked equally cold. "You'd be warmer if you came and sat next to me, conservation of heat and all that. We could put the blanket over us if you like."

Orlando didn't like. He was skittish enough in their own rooms and he positively bridled at the thought of appearing to be doing anything inappropriate in public, irrespective of whether the public were just three cows. But he sat down next to Jonty and they linked arms, which felt nice and safe.

"It's rather nice having introduced you to another innocent delight. I think you've actually quite enjoyed yourself, even if you're unlikely to admit it." Stewart smiled. "Glad we came?"

"I think so. For a physical activity, this has proved most cerebrally stimulating. Ow!" The last word had been in response to a whack on the shin from Jonty's boot.

"If I didn't hold you in the highest regard, I would take your *cerebrally stimulating* and do something with it that would make your hair stand on end." Stewart tried to look exasperated and failed. "You are the most aggravating man I've ever met, and the most wonderful. I think that I both love you and get annoyed with you in equal measure."

Orlando turned and stared at him. "What did you say?" He felt strange, almost sick, at the words he'd heard. He'd never expected them.

"I said that you're infuriating."

"No, you said something else, too. I want to hear you say it again." Orlando watched his friend, the man's emotions as usual playing across his face. He was obviously trying to recollect his words, probably spoken without too much thinking, as was usual with Stewart.

"I said that I both love you and get cross with you equally."

Coppersmith turned pale and studied his feet, the churning of his stomach becoming unbearable. "No one has ever said that they loved me; not even my mother. I don't think my father allowed her to." Orlando had never known such overt affection before and he'd no idea of how he was supposed to respond or what he should think or feel. He hoped that Stewart would be patient with him, that he'd recognize this was yet another thing that he was going to have to teach his friend about.

Jonty took Coppersmith's hand and rubbed it; though it was through the layers of leather and wool, there was plenty of intimacy present in the act. "I'm sure your parents did love you, my dearest friend, even if it wasn't spoken. Some people just find it too hard to say the actual words—costs too much, you see."

Lessons in Love

Orlando tightened his grip on Jonty's hands and smiled. He thought long and hard and at last found the words to explain himself. If Coppersmith ended up using the sort of language he might employ while he was teaching, he couldn't help himself. "I think I love you, too, Dr. Stewart although I've no definite proof. I can't believe that what I feel isn't love." And they kissed, as gently as if they'd never done such a thing before. For Coppersmith it felt even better than when they embraced back in the college, because now he knew that there was one person in the world who thought the world of him.

They sat for a while in silence, entirely content and sharing the odd kiss when the cows weren't looking, until the cold defeated even Stewart's determination. Turning the punt, they returned to *The White Hart* for a well earned pint, Coppersmith propelling the little craft all the way and Jonty sitting smiling, the pair of them in a glow of contentment.

On Thursday Stewart found a note in his pigeonhole from Inspector Wilson. It gave a wealth of information, primarily that the police had no further desire to talk to the Law student and the 'lurker' remained unfound. Sergeant Cohen had returned to work, preferring the bonhomie of the station to the lack of sympathy at home, (this information had been added to the bottom of the note in said officer's neat handwriting). They appreciated the fellows' continuing efforts to shed light on the mystery and reminded them not to put themselves in danger. Their own efforts were concentrated on investigating further those students without alibis and continuing their enquiries as to whether any similar, unsolved crimes had occurred anywhere else.

Orlando and Jonty read the note with disappointment. Stewart was keen to be *up and sleuthing* as he cheerfully put it, especially among his 'Monday group', but his friend urged continued caution. There was every chance they could find themselves talking to a murderer—what would be taken for friendly gossip and what would be construed as unwarranted interest? They bickered about this pre and post Hall, nearly came to a full blown argument, thought better of it and agreed in the end to meet the next afternoon to plan their next step.

Stewart was glad to get back to his rooms. Coppersmith had been frowning most of the evening and Jonty thought that he looked particularly gorgeous when he pulled that face. He wished the man wouldn't do it, especially when his own thoughts were always running along romantic lines at the moment, and when parts of his body were getting a bit frisky every time he was close to his lover. It was proving very frustrating, that all he ever got from Orlando was a kiss and a cuddle. Stewart found himself torn between the desire to force the issue a bit, take things further, and the need to preserve his friend's wonderful innocence, if simple innocence it was and not some deep-rooted aversion to bodily contact.

The revelation while they'd been punting had shocked him. Stewart had very affectionate parents who'd never left him in doubt that he was loved totally and without reservation, and if Coppersmith's family had never shown him such affection, then it was little wonder the man always seemed distressed when they were mentioned. And no wonder that he couldn't seem to commit himself physically.

At least Orlando had professed his love as well, and there was a glimmer of hope that Jonty wouldn't be spending the rest of his life celibate. But how they were ever going to deal with the matter of sex, Jonty couldn't begin to guess.

Friday afternoon and the floor of Coppersmith's living room was covered in newspapers and Jonty Stewart. Planning the next part of their investigation had dissolved into thin air, Stewart insisting that he needed time to think something through before he was even willing to discuss it.

Lessons in Love

Instead, the man was sprawled among the papers, monopolizing the fire as usual and chattering away to himself or Orlando or thin air, it didn't seem to matter much.

"Fascinating story in the local rag about a chap from the illustrious *college next door*." There was a tacit agreement among the fellows of St. Bride's not to mention their neighbor by name, probably stemming from time immemorial. "Says that this fellow, I mean *fellow* as opposed to chap, Orlando, do keep up and don't look so dim, had a wife in a cottage up on the Madingley Road. Kept it secret for years until he was eventually caught by a pair of undergraduates who had followed him thinking he was a spy, although who they thought he was spying for they couldn't say. I think that they were mathematics students and believed that the man was one of Bonaparte's agents."

"Very funny, Jonty. I happen to know that they were from the School of English and suspected him of working for the enemies of Queen Elizabeth. None of them realize she's been dead these three hundred years."

Stewart screwed up a sheet of paper and bounced it off Coppersmith's head. "Idiot. I'm bored, Orlando, I need something to do." He glanced up at the window, but the rain was still streaming down the panes. "Can't go for a walk, don't want to play Sherlock Holmes at the moment, fed up with tea and buns. Bored."

"Shall we wander down to the museum and look at the Sedgwick collection, you always enjoy that…"

Another ball of paper glanced off Orlando's skull. "If I see another piece of ichthyosaur, or whatever the blessed thing is, this side of Lammas, I'll probably impale myself with it. And I don't want to look at the paintings in the Fitzwilliam and it's too wet for the Botanic Gardens and I don't want to read a book." He lay on his back, hands behind his head, eyes closed. "Bored."

Orlando frowned. "If you think that making all this fuss

is going to cause me to come over there and indulge in romantic activity, you have another think coming." Something Coppersmith particularly liked about his friend was the way that his thoughts played across his face, as easily read as a book. And his face clearly said *Bugger, I've been rumbled.*

Jonty slightly raised his head and opened one eye. "What a wonderful idea Orlando, never thought of that before, splendid way to beat the ennui." One of the paper missiles made a reappearance, bouncing off Jonty's head this time, Coppersmith having a surprisingly swift and accurate arm. "I'm not sure I ever want to kiss you again after being in that punt on Wednesday. I think that embracing you and freezing off vital parts of my body are now inextricably linked in my brain." He sat up, took off his spectacles, and cleared the broadsheets away into a fairly neat pile, thrusting it under a chair. "Come down here and join me. You could warm up some of the parts that suffered so much from the cold."

Orlando rose slowly and dropped down next to him, just a bit disappointed that Jonty's reading glasses had been put away. In some strange way the things made his friend one hundred and forty seven per cent more attractive. At least. "I remember what happened last time we sat in front of the fire—last Saturday in your rooms, Jonty." He actually had only a vague recollection, the alcohol having made the remembrance rather hazy. But he knew it had been good.

"But of course you remember—it was wonderful." Stewart reached out his hand to stroke his friend's face. "Would you be interested in a repeat performance?"

"You know that I would, as long as you also understand that I don't want to do *those things*." Orlando shut his eyes and shuddered. As far as he was concerned Lord Morcar's books had been full of filth and he didn't want anything to do with such stuff. When he'd been a young man, the total extent of his preparation for matters sexual had been his father teaching him that he should take a cold bath should

Lessons in Love

he become aroused in any way. He'd never had to obey the instruction. And Orlando had no idea what Jonty had been taught, but he'd assumed it was something similar.

Stewart took his friend's hand, speaking slowly and gently. "Orlando, I really do think that you should tell me exactly what you read in those books."

Coppersmith told him, in detail, becoming paler and paler with every word. It all seemed even more disgraceful when spoken aloud.

"Would you be very upset to know that *I* had done some of *those things*, Orlando?"

"Jonty?" Coppersmith didn't know whether he was upset or not, just incredibly shocked. He knew that Stewart had much more experience of the world in general than he did, but he'd always assumed that his friend was the same as him in this regard. Still a virgin. "I had no idea."

"You wouldn't—I've never given you the slightest intimation. Do you want me to tell you about it?"

Coppersmith nodded, rather reluctantly. He wasn't sure he was ready to be confronted with yet another example of the realities of life.

"Orlando, I'd have had to tell you at some point. We should have no secrets. I also think that you should understand that what you read in those bloody books isn't how it always is. They seem to be full of people taking advantage of each other, forcing their desires on unwilling partners and being almost bestial. It doesn't have to be like that, it shouldn't be like that. Sex can be shared, enjoyed equally without coercion. I actually have knowledge of both things."

Coppersmith moved closer to his friend, laying his head on Stewart's chest and snuggling down into a position of comfort and security—he always felt safe when he had Jonty's arms around him. He'd constantly feared the unknown, things you couldn't analyze and quantify, and this was totally uncharted territory. "Please tell me."

"I was at boarding school, Orlando. You, being a day

boy, may well have had very little notion about what went on when lessons were over and lights put out. The things you read about in your books, some of them happened to me, frequently and against my will, and I could find no help. The Housemaster seemed content to turn a blind eye. He probably would have joined in were he brave enough." Stewart trembled, bit his lip.

Coppersmith turned his face up to his friend's; he hated to see such pain in Stewart's eyes. He wondered whether Jonty had hoped to keep all this secret from him and supposed the man had been left with no other choice than to bare his soul. The thought of Stewart being used so cruelly filled Coppersmith full of vengeful thoughts and something else that he'd never felt before—a small spark of warmth in his stomach. Or lower than his stomach if he was being honest. "Jonty, how did you ever survive?"

Stewart took a deep breath before he answered; Orlando could imagine the man's body drawing on all his courage. "Because that's what you just have to do, Orlando. Survive. Call on your inner reserves of strength, apply the stiff upper lip, enjoy the good things that do come your way in between. I don't want to talk about it now, it's done and I just want to forget about it." He gave another huge sigh. "Anyway, when I came up to St. Bride's, I was determined to put school behind me. I thought I might find myself a nice girl somewhere, but that was a daft idea. I like girls, but I've never wanted to give one of them more than a peck on the cheek. And then I met Richard."

Coppersmith froze. He could deal in his mind with the actions of unnamed boys at school, channeling his anger at them for the hideous acts they had forced upon his own Jonty, but a specific person, here in *his* college was another prospect. "Was...Richard," Orlando thought that he might choke on the name, "was he another undergraduate?"

"Yes, in the year above me. He looked so much like you do, Orlando, I think that's why I took such a shine to you that first evening here. Frighteningly clever, too, and that

Lessons in Love

reminds me of you as well." Jonty ran his fingers through his friend's curls. "I think he saved my life. Oh, I don't mean that I was contemplating throwing myself in the Cam, but I was feeling so low, after the realization that there was no point in looking for a potential Mrs. Stewart, as I only wanted another *Mr.* Stewart and where was I going to find one?"

Coppersmith reached for the hand in his hair, brought it to his lips. "You've found one here, Jonty." The more Orlando thought about other men touching *his* Jonty, the more the peculiar tingling in his groin started to nag at him.

"I know I have, Orlando and I'm eternally grateful. But you must know that Richard was my first love, even though you will be my last. I loved him, spiritually and physically. With Richard things were so nice, he was so gentle, and when he died I thought that my world had come to an end."

Coppersmith looked up again at Stewart's face, noticing the tears and the sad, wistful look he'd not seen there since he first took Jonty to his rooms, the night the women invaded. He desperately wanted to say that he was sorry, but he wasn't—if Richard had lived, then Stewart wouldn't be his. Still, he had to say something. "How did he die?"

"TB. He caught it from some poor hapless soul when he was out helping at the soup kitchen. Richard used to go out with the Salvation Army when he was at home; he felt this desperate need to look after people, that's why he was reading medicine. That's why he took up with me." Jonty's tears now started to flow unhindered. "I don't deceive myself that he might have really loved me, I know that he didn't, but I believe that he felt the closest thing to love that he could manage. And when he was gone, I was convinced that I would never again feel such affection for anyone." He caressed Coppersmith's cheek. "Got that wrong, too, didn't I?"

Orlando had experienced envy just once before, when Jonty had been out with his colleagues from the School of English, but that wasn't like the jealousy he was enraged with now. He wanted to get hold of all the men who had ever laid hands on his friend and tear them limb from limb with his bare hands, Richard included. He was horrified that anyone else would have had the temerity to touch that blessed body, kiss those precious lips. Now the feeling in his groin had turned to a burning and was making itself known physically; he was uncomfortable and hoped that Stewart wouldn't notice. He tried to concentrate on the conversation, although it was proving difficult. "Do you really mean that I will be your last love, Jonty? What if anything happened to me?"

"Then I'd end up like most of the fellows here, immersed in my studies to the exclusion of all else, and celibate for the rest of my life, probably. It costs too much to love, Orlando and there comes a limit to how much I'm prepared to spend." The tears had stopped now. Jonty borrowed Coppersmith's hankie to blow his nose and managed a smile.

There was still something nagging at Orlando's brain and it had to be resolved, even though he was dreading the answer. Morcar's books had spoken enough about men who needed to be satisfied. Without Richard, what might Jonty have resorted to? "Did you ever think of visiting the sort of boys that Morcar did? After Richard died, I mean."

Stewart shook his head. "No, not once. I can't separate physical love from spiritual, like many men seem to be able to. Can't *do anything* if I don't feel very deeply for the other person. So it's just Richard and you, Orlando, not some great, long string of dalliances and flirtations."

Coppersmith was immensely relieved about that, but would have been even happier if there had been no Richard. It was going to take a long time to get that young man out of his mind. When he came to analyze the afternoon, afterwards—as he analyzed everything in his life to try to make sense of it—he realized it was at this point that he'd made up his mind. He was going to defy his father, there would be no cold baths or repression of feelings. His body

Lessons in Love

was telling him that he wanted to be as intimate with Jonty as Richard had been and he was going to make it happen, some way or another. He took his friend's hand to kiss it, finger by finger, taking each digit into his mouth in turn. He hoped that Stewart would find this simple gesture as ridiculously arousing as he did.

"Orlando, I really don't think that you know what you're doing."

"On the contrary, for once in my life I think that I know exactly what I am trying to do." Coppersmith was never one to go back once he'd made a decision. He desired Jonty Stewart and he was going to pull him closer, kiss him fiercely, press their bodies as tightly together as he could. As soon as their bodies touched, it was obvious to Orlando that Jonty was every bit as excited as he was and that things might well reach their natural conclusion very soon. They continued to kiss, Orlando full of wildness and desperation, their bodies writhing against one another.

When he thought about it later that night, Coppersmith tried to find words to describe what was going on, but maths had left him poor in the essential vocabulary. It was a tingling, a burning, like a small spark igniting tinder in a room full of gunpowder, making a fire that grew and grew until the whole thing made a blinding explosion. At the time all he knew was that he needed to press himself up against Jonty, to writhe and rub until the pain, the longing, was eased, satisfied. And when it happened, when the shattering detonation came, he couldn't understand why it felt so good and so painful, why he wanted it to stop now, before he was consumed by ecstasy, and why he never wanted it to stop at all.

That magnificent ending came within an extremely short time, Orlando lacking the experience and Jonty the willpower for either of them to exert any self-control. A few mad kisses, two bodies straddling each other's legs and pounding, pressing, was all that it had seemed to take, no time for even taking off their clothes. Coppersmith lay back afterwards, unspeaking, completely devastated. Stewart, turned to face him, seemed to wait for him to say something, perhaps afraid to speak himself unless he made some awful blunder. In the end he could probably restrain himself no longer; Jonty was rarely silent for long. "Not bad, was it, Orlando?"

"You have an enormous capacity for understatement, Jonty. I've never experienced anything like that before." He hadn't. It had felt like his whole body was being ripped apart and even now little waves of pleasure were rippling through him.

Stewart sniggered. "Oh, this was hardly anything, Orlando. It can be so much better than that."

Coppersmith stared in disbelief. Jonty had to be lying, there could be nothing better than what he'd felt. That was like saying that there was a number larger than infinity. "And would you be happy for us to do this again, Jonty?"

"Well, not immediately, Orlando, takes a bit of time to recover, you know."

Coppersmith landed a whack on the Stewart rump. "Not now, you clown." He lay back on the floor and closed his eyes, savoring the last little sensations before they ebbed away entirely. "I think it'll take me days to recover. *And* I'll have to resign my fellowship, Jonty. I think I'm incapable of having another rational mathematical thought ever again."

Stewart sniggered again. "You should have studied English, Dr. Coppersmith, this is just the sort of thing to greatly increase one's understanding of the works of Donne or Lovelace. Half the reason the dunderheads can't grasp the essentials of the Bard is that they have no real experience of life, in all its glories and tragedies. Perhaps the college should consider making 'romantic activity' a compulsory part of the syllabus?"

Orlando began to formulate arguments against this, realized he was being gulled and walloped Stewart's behind again. Jonty giggled, removed his posterior from smacking

Lessons in Love

range and looked up at the window. "Rain's cleared up nicely, Dr. Coppersmith, we've still time to get ourselves cleaned up and go for a walk along the river before Chapel."

"Chapel? How can we?" Orlando looked horrified, "after…it wouldn't be right."

"And you don't even believe in God. How can you be so skittish?"

"As I've told you before, Jonty, I'm agnostic, not atheist. I merely wish for proof."

Stewart snorted.

"And I'm not skittish. It just seems rather blasphemous to go to Choral Evensong after…" He could feel himself blushing and knew that Jonty was watching him with interest, probably to see what awkward euphemism he'd find to describe what they'd just done. Well, he could wait in vain—Coppersmith stayed deliberately silent. There were no words that he could comfortably use.

"If it's blasphemy to go to Evensong afterwards, then it was just as wrong to do it in the first place. We're as much in God's sight here as we are in the Chapel. I for one simply find it impossible to believe that any expression of loyal and faithful love is wrong. I think it's better to be here with you than be at home with a respectable wife and a string of mistresses. Plenty of men would be happy enough to go straight from the arms of their paramours to sit in the family pew with their lawful spouse."

Orlando considered. "Yes, that would be worse." He suddenly hit on a happy thought. "And if we had been sinful, the best place to go would be somewhere we could make our confessions, wouldn't it?"

Jonty hooted with laughter. "You're starting to sound just like one of the idiots I have to supervise. You were absolutely right in saying that you'd lost your capacity for rational thought, at least for the moment. I'm going to go to Choral Evensong and give thanks to God for sending me such an adorable idiot to love. And I will dutifully say my confession as I always do, but I for one don't feel sinful, not about this, anyway." He glanced slyly at his friend, "not like I feel about stealing the last of your Liquorice Allsorts."

Coppersmith was horrified. "You swore that wasn't you. You said *I'd* eaten it and forgotten."

"Then I'd better include lying in my confession, too, hadn't I?" Jonty smiled sweetly then looked suddenly serious. "And when we come to the final collect, I'll be thinking of both us and St. Bride's. We've had a lovely afternoon, Orlando, but the threat in this college remains."

Lighten our darkness we beseech thee Oh God and by thy great mercy defend us from all perils and dangers of this night...

Chapter Eight

Saturday morning and a very smugly satisfied Jonty Stewart was watching the watery sunshine making a valiant effort to penetrate into his bedroom. *It* had happened. Well, *something* had happened and if it wasn't quite the consummation he'd devoutly wished for, it had been pretty special. He nestled down into the warm bed and tried to relive every little moment of the afternoon before, despite the nagging thoughts that kept knocking at the door of his conscience for attention.

Mackenzie, Trumper, Ingleby. There was something about one or more of those students that needed further investigation, although Jonty had nothing but instinct, and the lack of alibis, on which to base his assumption. Even though he didn't depend on the reliability of alibis as much as Orlando did.

Orlando, his own Dr. Coppersmith, had got so very jealous the day before. Jonty had realized that fact as soon as he'd started to talk about Richard, and what an amazing effect that envy had. Where gentle romance consistently failed to have an effect, plain jealousy had succeeded amazingly. Stewart indulged in another few priceless memories of precious minutes, until less pleasant events reared their heads again.

The 'lurker', whoever he was, still roamed the college. Stewart's instinct was torn between suspecting him immediately as the murderer and dismissing him as another irrelevance in a case that had already seen two students entered as suspects and as soon discarded. Even Coppersmith was convinced that if the 'lurker' was identified, the case would be solved. He'd said as much when he'd been trying to make Jonty discuss the affair yesterday.

Yesterday. Not even eighteen hours since they had managed to overcome the fear that had been nagging at Orlando since he read those stupid books. Stewart had been immensely relieved to find out that Orlando was no ascetic; the man had simply needed a threat to his possession to prompt him into action. All sorts of possibilities opened up now, if only *someone* didn't think too much about what they'd done and what they still might do.

There was no chance of Coppersmith *not* thinking. He was at that very moment lying on his own settee, woken early and unable to sleep again, drinking hot, strong coffee and considering everything that had happened on Friday afternoon in minute detail. From the way Jonty's nose had crinkled when he'd been crying, to the rapture on his face when *it* had happened. Orlando was not yet sure how he should refer to *it,* even in his thoughts. Most of the terms he knew had been used in *those* books and were therefore not worthy of being an appropriate name for such a marvelous event.

He would have been appalled had he realized how his celebrated powers of logic weren't applying themselves to this. Some of what happened in Morcar's books was not a million miles away from what had occurred in Orlando's own rooms, but the formidable Coppersmith brain refused

Lessons in Love

to connect the two. He felt that he and Jonty were like two innocents exploring some romantic Garden of Eden and that all they did was pure and untainted. He was in love and he was illogical with it.

Once he was up and fed, Stewart decided that he had to make a trip to the stationers. He had cakes and sherry in abundance in his rooms, but barely a sniff of blue ink or decent sized paper. He wandered off into town with half his mind on whether he needed some new pencils, the other half still in front of Orlando's fire and none of it on where he was going, which was why he walked straight into Trumper and Jackson. They were laden with groceries and seemed to be planning a trip to the South Pole given the supplies that they had amassed.

"Sorry, Dr. Stewart," they announced in unison.

"No, my fault entirely, I was woolgathering as usual." He eyed their shopping bags. "Not giving you large enough portions at Hall?"

"Oh, no." Trumper assured him. "Having a lunch party with some of the chaps. You know, Mackenzie, Ingleby, loads of them."

"I see that you've got plenty of lemonade. Handy if the tummy plays up again after over-indulging in this lot…"

"Oh yes." Jackson pulled a face at the memory of it.

Stewart smiled. His own nurse had sworn by the medicinal properties of boiled lemonade and ghastly it had tasted, too. He wasn't sure if the drink worked from its own virtues or from the threat of having to take it again if no recovery followed. "You mentioned Ingleby?" He raised his eyebrows, "is that our friend with the unusual theories about these murders?"

Jackson snorted. "We say that he's got eyes and ears like two rag and bone men, going around picking up all sorts of rubbish. He and Mackenzie gossip akin to a pair of old biddies. It's amusing for a while, but it can be wearing."

He looked at Trumper and gained a nod of agreement.

"Absolutely, Dr. Stewart. He caused all that trouble for that poor Law student, didn't he?" Trumper rolled his eyes in a rather theatrical display of disapproval.

"Well, let's hope that they can confine themselves to more agreeable subjects, shall we? Enjoy your lunch, gentlemen." Jonty turned on his heel and sauntered off to the stationers with the little phrase *goes around picking up all sorts of rubbish* nagging at him.

It soon appeared that he might as well rearrange his supervision venue to Kings Parade, as another one of this particular quartet managed to walk straight into him. "Sorry sir," Mackenzie bowed slightly in deference. His arms were full of books, none of them, Jonty noted, likely to be of any use on his course.

"This city is coming to something when a chap can't walk along the road without his students assaulting him." Stewart produced what he hoped was a look of mock affront. "Just had Trumper and his pal Jackson trying to throw pâté and petit fours all over me. Guess Ingleby will try to run me down on his bicycle next."

Mackenzie snorted. "No chance, Dr. Stewart. Far too early for him, he rarely sees the light of day before noon. Probably have to pour him out of bed and into Jackson's rooms and I don't know how I'll get a razor onto him." He bowed again and sauntered off, whistling, leaving Jonty now nagged by the notion of Ingleby sleeping late. Was he keeping late hours as the 'lurker'? Stewart would have to put that thought past Orlando, if he ever managed to evade English students for long enough to get some ruddy ink.

The two fellows of Bride's spent Saturday afternoon discussing whether Ingleby might be the mysterious observer of college events. Coppersmith suggested a trap—waiting together for several hours each night until they should glimpse the 'lurker' and then endeavoring to catch him. Stewart didn't agree with that particular plan, wanting to be in his own warm bed, or Orlando's, which was preferable although highly unlikely. Anyway, the 'lurker' must have twigged that the police were onto him. There'd been a buzz of rumor throughout the college these last few days and he was likely to be lying low for the time being.

They tired of talking and getting nowhere so, deciding on a walk along the river, they scrambled into hats, coats and gloves—as fit for the East Anglian weather that Ferguson found so mild—and set off. As they passed one of the stairways, they met Trumper and Jackson's guests, who were easily recognizable by their sober yet satisfied countenances. Mackenzie was dashing off, *to go for a run before hall, Dr. Stewart, it sets up the appetite so*. Ingleby didn't seem to have any clear plans and so was being dragged along by the rest of the lads in the direction of the Junior Common Room, some of them mumbling about setting up a game of draughts. As they left, Orlando noticed a small object had appeared on the ground. He picked it up, inspected it and then let Jonty do the same.

"What do you make of this?"

"It's a badge, Orlando, that's all, probably to denote membership of some society. I dare say one of the dunderheads dropped it. I'll ask around at Monday's supervision." He slipped the shiny little thing into his pocket and forgot all about it.

Saturday evening came and they slunk off to The Bishop's Cope, having excused themselves high table on the grounds that they'd been diligently helping the police and needed a break. Stewart realized that Hall had been a sore trial to Coppersmith on the Friday evening, the man being terrified that the rest of the fellows would somehow know exactly what he and Jonty had been up to during the afternoon. This despite Jonty's repeated hissed assurances that there was no obvious outward sign, no raddle mark or the like, that would announce that they'd been *at it*.

Orlando seemed certainly more at ease in the warm,

smoky atmosphere of the bar and began to show a degree of perkiness. They supped, they drank (but not to excess, *just in case*), then returned to college and Coppersmith's room in a warm haze of roast chicken and Abbott's ale.

"No port tonight, Orlando," Stewart raised his hand to decline his friend's offer of a nightcap. "Other business to attend to."

Coppersmith looked puzzled, causing Jonty to pull him closer and look winningly into his deep brown eyes. "Unless you've forgotten about yesterday, of course, or aren't you sufficiently recovered yet?"

Orlando smirked. It was a smug little grin, the first genuinely lascivious one that Stewart had ever seen on his friend's face.

"Oh, so we haven't forgotten?"

"Not likely to, it's etched permanently on my mind, the afternoon Jonty Stewart seduced me."

Stewart giggled. "Seem to remember it was you doing the seducing, Orlando. Very out of character." He ventured a kiss and was delighted by the passionate way in which it was responded to. His eager little fingers started to attack the buttons of Coppersmith's waistcoat, distracting his victim with a simultaneous assault on his ear. Orlando could be made almost insensible if he got the right part of his ear and molested it, a useful tactic when he wanted to move from waistcoat buttons to shirt buttons, which is exactly what Stewart's hands were doing. A surprise offensive on Coppersmith's neck allowed Jonty's fingers to insinuate themselves into the gaps he had created, finding soft skin through the thin, silky vest and caressing it into goosebumps. He was surprised and delighted that there was no resistance from Orlando, just a gentle crooning and a sudden, "Should we go to my bed, Jonty?"

Seven simple words, none of them above one syllable, apart from his name, but complicated enough to make the world spin around Stewart. For possibly the first time in his life he lost the ability to speak and had to acquiesce with a

Lessons in Love

simple nod of the head. And so it was Coppersmith who led *him* by the hand into the little bedroom, a room that he'd only ever glimpsed before. Orlando began to take off Jonty's jacket and pullover, gently and with a strange respectfulness, almost as if he were a valet rather than a lover. The buttons of the shirt were undone tenderly and both this and Stewart's vest removed with great care, folded neatly with the other things over a chair. Coppersmith barely touched skin in the process and Jonty found it much more stimulating than if his friend had been caressing him. He felt hot and cold all over, not daring to speak in case his voice betrayed him or he began to make all sorts of suggestions that would scare Coppersmith off.

Jonty eventually found his voice. "Let me help you now, Orlando." He set to work on those of Coppersmith's buttons which had eluded him before, deliberately casting the clothes he removed onto the floor in an untidy heap as an act of defiance, concentrating his tension and height of emotion into the scattering of shirt and vest. And still not a kiss nor a touch had passed between them since they entered the little room. Stewart sat down on the bed to remove his shoes and socks, filled again with the dread of appearing ridiculous and Orlando followed suit, much to his friend's relief. At least he was to be spared the sight of Coppersmith in nothing but black socks, an apparition that would have made him giggle uncontrollably and broken the fragile romantic mood they'd created. Orlando obviously wanted a repeat of the day before and Jonty was desperate to oblige him, but still the thought nagged at the back of his head that Coppersmith might remember *the books* and get cold feet. Colder than the ones that trod on the St. Bride's linoleum.

"Get in the bed, Jonty, we mustn't let you freeze." Orlando pulled back the covers—clean linen sheets that smelled of lavender, topped with thick blankets, not standard college issue. Stewart crept in, moving across to leave plenty of room for his friend. Coppersmith hesitated. "Should I put out the light?" A little gas mantle glowed brightly from the other room and filled the bedroom with warm half tones.

"No. I want to see you, Orlando. Want to be sure that it *is* you." Jonty didn't need to finish the sentence, he knew his friend would understand. But it was puzzling him why it was taking his lover so long to get into the bed.

At last Coppersmith turned round, slipped between the covers and landed a small, innocent kiss on Jonty's waiting lips. Stewart sighed and snuggled his head onto Orlando's chest. "Do you want us to sleep together or lie together? I'm so happy now, just having you so close to me, that either of them would be a delight."

"Both, Jonty. It would simply break my heart to share the pleasures of yesterday again only to have you leave me afterwards." Orlando fingered Jonty's little crucifix as it glittered faintly in the light from the mantle, his body's shyness belying the eager words he'd used.

"Have to leave at some point, Orlando. Can't let the bedder find my room not slept in. Early morning would do." Jonty turned his face up to his friend's and began to kiss him, gently at first, then with more passion, letting his hands begin an exploration of Coppersmith's lean and lovely body. He'd always kept his investigations strictly north of the Equator but tonight he was going to risk the ceremony of crossing the line, in search of the rare undiscovered delights of Orlando's southern hemisphere. His fingers moved southwards, along the line of Coppersmith's chest, finding breast and nipple. He was relieved to discover that his lover responded in kind, as usual by a clumsy copy of what Jonty was doing, but that didn't matter. Orlando was trying hard to learn what to do and he'd soon be brave enough to try some ideas of his own.

Stewart kept kissing his lover's mouth and face and neck, savoring the unique tang of Coppersmith's flesh, something which tasted sweeter than Richard's ever had. One hand caressed Orlando's ear, while the other wormed downwards and gradually came closer to one of the more intimate parts of Coppersmith's anatomy. He was delighted that Orlando squeaked, literally squeaked, with something that might be surprise or pleasure or simply indignation, when Jonty made contact with the sturdy peninsular he'd found south of the man's navel. But he drew his hand away and waited for the repercussions; this might have been a step too far.

"Are we allowed to touch each other like that, Jonty?" Coppersmith's breaths came short and sharp.

"Don't you like it?"

"How could anyone not like it? It's like agony and joy all wrapped up together." Even by the faint light Coppersmith looked mystified. "I just can't believe something so gratifying can be right."

Stewart couldn't contain the giggles he'd so dreaded. "Well, of course it's right. This isn't like chess, there are no rules written down anywhere, Orlando. It's up to us to decide what we want." Jonty moved his hand back to where it had caused such a reaction and found that Coppersmith's body spoke more readily than his words did.

Orlando nestled into the curve that Stewart's muscular frame had made, pressing himself close and tentatively making fresh explorations of his own. "You make the rules, Jonty. I think I'd feel safe if you said what was right and wrong."

"We don't need to make any rules, Orlando. Just do what you feel, and if you're not comfortable, tell me, please." He looked penetratingly into his friend's eyes, concerned that he didn't want to force anything upon such a precious innocent. "You will tell me?"

Coppersmith nodded, expressing his agreement in a long, lazy kiss that made Jonty shiver with anticipation.

It took longer to reach the perfect ending this time. Everything was less desperate than it had been the day before and gentle touches began to achieve with more languor what frantic bodily contact had done so rapidly.

They stroked, they caressed, they squeezed, Orlando faithfully mirroring whatever was being done to him. Stewart was sure he was just following along, trying to reproduce in his friend the feelings that Jonty was engendering in him. But it worked, it worked beautifully, and the bliss they shared, almost simultaneously, was beyond all anticipation. It had been nice making love to Richard; with Orlando it was astounding.

It was so dazzling it even made Jonty speechless for a while, though, inevitably, not that long. "Told you it could be even better, didn't I? I may have lied about the last of the Liquorice Allsorts, but I wouldn't lie about this." Stewart snuggled his head onto Orlando's chest and sighed.

"Never doubted you for a moment, Jonty." Coppersmith squeezed his friend tightly to him and grinned. "May not ever trust you with my sweets again, but I'll trust you with my body forever."

If understanding comes in visions, both men found it that night as they lay contentedly sleeping in each other's arms. Orlando dreamed that a number larger than infinity—several numbers, each more amazing than the others—definitely did exist and he, Orlando Coppersmith, had been the first to discover them. He'd gone on to win the Nobel Prize for Mathematics, despite the fact that there wasn't one, and had announced to the world that he dedicated it to Stewart for giving him the key to the discovery.

Jonty dreamed of Richard, as he'd done on and off these last few years, though rarely since he'd met Orlando. In his dream, Richard was waving goodbye and Jonty was no longer sad about it.

They didn't sleep together on the Sunday night. At eleven o'clock on Sunday morning a third body was found and chaos once more reigned in St. Bride's.

One of the law students had left chapel and gone to find Marchbanks, the loud mouthed young man whom Ingleby

Lessons in Love

had told the police about and whose absence from the morning service the student had noticed and worried over. The usual pattern emerged; the door to the room was open and the window, too, the body was disheveled, death had been by strangulation and the spiteful note was firmly in place.

And the usual pattern followed. The arrival of the porters, the Master and the police in short order. Wilson and Cohen were both no doubt disgruntled to be dragged from the traditional Sunday domestic smells of roast beef and Yorkshire pudding being cooked, food that they were not likely to taste this day. Here was another scene to be fully investigated on the slight hope that this either very clever or very lucky murderer had left a calling card of some description. There was the prospect of another set of alibis to be gone through, although the police decided early on to concentrate on those students who couldn't adequately account for themselves on the previous occasions. And there was now certainty that the culprit came from within the college, as the main gate was guarded as if the crown jewels themselves were resident at St. Bride's.

Hall carried on as normal, but very few of those present could do justice to the excellent beef, not even Dr. Stewart, who for once didn't manage to clear his plate. The place was abuzz with the latest news and the fellows weren't discussing Morton's fork, but 'The St. Bride's Strangler' as some tasteless wit had named him, probably some idiot from *the college next door*.

Jonty went off on some mysterious business of his own soon after pudding had been served, and largely left uneaten, leaving Orlando to wander back alone to the SCR for coffee. Stewart soon rejoined his companion and simply said that he expected the police would join them in his rooms a little later on. They found no relaxation or pleasure in their usual surroundings this afternoon, so, quickly draining their cups, they sought the refuge of Stewart's set and considered this new development.

It was well gone three o'clock by the time Wilson and Cohen appeared and almost immediately Stewart disappeared, exchanging knowing looks with the policemen and leaving Coppersmith to entertain them. He crashed back through the door not long afterwards, bearing a tray with covered plates. Like a conjurer reaching the climax of his best trick, he pulled off the lids to reveal two full roast dinners, both of them hot and smelling delicious. Two smaller covered plates hinted at apple pie and custard.

"Find a bottle of something will you, Orlando? I know that these gentlemen are on duty but I'm sure that they'll indulge our hospitality."

The gentlemen were more than happy to indulge their hosts, having anticipated a late lunch of nothing more exciting than bread and cheese. Just how Jonty had worked this trick, Coppersmith couldn't be sure, but he guessed that Stewart had wielded his charm in the vicinity of the college cooks, most of whom were female, matronly and easy targets for a pretty face and winning smile. *That man's dangerous,* thought Orlando. *He could get anything he wanted at any time with a smile like that.* He remembered exactly what Jonty had got from him the night before and put his attention to opening the bottle of claret before anyone noticed how red he'd turned.

Facts about the latest murder emerged from the policemen between mouthfuls of roast potatoes. They'd found no new clue, but they did have a tangible link to the second murder. An initial survey of Marchbanks' personal effects gave nothing away, but a little cache, which was located by Cohen, who had a 'nose' for these things, contained some love letters, all signed R-C and in a handwriting that matched the second victim's. They made it clear where Russell-Clarke had taken his pleasures.

Coppersmith felt very puzzled. "But why should Marchbanks have made such remarks as he did? Why make yourself look like a potential suspect?"

Wilson, Stewart and Cohen all exchanged knowing

Lessons in Love

glances, which made Orlando rather self conscious and not a little cross.

"Have you never seen 'Hamlet', Coppersmith?" Jonty piped up. "*The lady doth protest too much, methinks* and all that?"

Wilson seemed to take pity on the mathematician and explained. "A smoke screen, sir. People often hide their true nature by condemning the like in public as loudly as possible. Mr. Cohen did have his suspicions about that when we spoke to him, but I wasn't convinced." He looked suddenly very serious. "I wish that I had been."

"And are we any closer to a solution?" Dr. Stewart sounded despondent and Coppersmith eyed him with concern. This business was affecting all their lives and everyone at St. Bride's seemed to be going around with one eye over their shoulder, whether they were likely victims or not. Jonty must have realized the effect his question might have on the constabulary and apologized. "I hope you'll forgive me gentlemen, I know that you're doing all you can. It's just that we're under enormous strain." He put his hands into his pockets and went to look out the window, only then finding the little badge that had turned up the day before. "Oh, I do believe that we were going to give you this." He passed the object over to Wilson, who suddenly had a gleam in his eye.

"And where did this little beauty turn up?"

"Out of the pocket of one of the undergraduates here, we think." Coppersmith cut in and related all that he and Stewart had discussed the day before about the little bunch of English students, and how they'd found the badge on the ground when the party they'd encountered had dispersed. "Is it important?" Orlando noted the glint that had now appeared in Cohen's eye, too.

"Lord Morcar's family contacted us after his effects had been returned. There was an item missing, a small badge which was associated with his membership of a dining society at Eton. The lad treasured the thing and it had great sentimental value to his mother. Well, from the description she gave us, we'll be able to return it to her, if not just yet."

They all sat for a moment as the import of this little shining piece of metal sank in.

"Someone had taken it from his room, possibly from the body itself?" Stewart stated the obvious, but he felt that someone had to.

"We can't jump to that conclusion, Dr. Stewart." Cohen smiled indulgently. "We must keep an open mind, and we must get to talk to all those young men as soon as possible." He and Wilson rose, another weary slog ahead for them and their officers. They expressed their gratitude for the food and the continued help, made the usual warning about taking care—expected it to be ignored—and departed.

Jonty sighed wearily and motioned to the door himself. "Mind if I get some time to myself? Got a pile of essays still to work through for tomorrow, Orlando. Been led astray a bit the last few days." He produced the merest hint of a grin. "Probably won't go to high table, I seem to have lost my appetite."

"Are you feeling quite well?" Coppersmith had never known Stewart to be off his fodder and was worried that this new occurrence was due not to the third murder but to what they'd done last night, when he'd practically dragged the man to his bed. Perhaps Jonty was regretting the whole thing.

"I'm quite well, Orlando." Jonty must have recognized his friend's concern and smiled. "It really is just this whole business getting me down. There's a limit to any man's store of *joie de vie*, even Jonty Stewart's." He drew Coppersmith's brow down to his lips and gently kissed it. "I'll see you tomorrow before dinner. Come round to my rooms and we'll take a glass of sherry."

"I do love you, Jonty. Don't forget it."

"I won't, Orlando. It's one of the few things keeping me optimistic at present. Goodnight."

"And lock your door..." came echoing up the stairs as

Lessons in Love

the sound of footsteps clattered down.

Chapter Nine

Monday afternoon and far from there being sherry on Dr. Stewart's table there was dried mud and other filth in abundance. "What are you up to?" Coppersmith had knocked and entered the set of rooms, rather cross that the door hadn't been locked, but his intended words of caution had died away on observing the strange sight.

"Cleaning the old rugby boots." Dr. Stewart's tongue protruded from his mouth as he concentrated on removing some ancient pieces of mud and grass. "The chaps from the School of History have challenged us to a game and they always have a habit of slaughtering the English lecturers. Chaps heard I got my blue and they've roped me in, at scrum half, I'm pleased to say."

"When are you playing?"

"Wednesday afternoon, down at St. Thomas' sports ground. Fancy coming to watch? Might even get you a game if you wanted, the team could do with a bit of pace down the wing, or so I'm told. We could always pretend you were an expert on Jane Austen." Jonty put his head to one side like a little bird. "You look like someone who could talk very knowledgeably about Mr. D'Arcy."

Lessons in Love

Coppersmith wasn't sure whether this was a compliment but couldn't be bothered to pursue it. "I'm afraid I gave up rugger long ago. Snapped an Achilles' tendon—bloody painful it was, so don't snigger—and I was always worried it would go again. I assumed that you'd given up the game, too."

"Oh, no. I was playing regularly up until last year. Then the biggest and ugliest forward I've ever seen, he played for the Royal College of Science where I suspect he was one of the objects for study rather than one of the students, knocked me out cold. Got concussion and the doctor said I wasn't to play for six months. Well, I'm a week or two short but who cares?"

Orlando desperately wanted to say that *he* cared, that he had no desire for Stewart to hurt himself, but he'd learned not to argue with his friend once he'd made up his mind to do something. Jonty always won that particular game. "Give me one of them." Coppersmith picked up the boot with evident distaste. "Didn't you clean them the last time you wore them?"

"Well, sort of, but I had rather a stinker of a headache at the time, Orlando, and blurred vision. This was the best I could manage..." Stewart looked appealingly at his friend, who sighed with resignation and got to work with the brush. He had little doubt that he was being conned, that Jonty knew, if he played his cards right, Coppersmith would have those boots looking spotless again by the time came around for high table and not a bit of Stewart elbow grease expended. But he was feeling generous towards his friend at the moment, not least because of the wonderful time they'd had on Saturday night.

"Care for a sherry, Orlando?" Stewart poured out two glasses and laid them out of range of the flying mud.

"I would love one, if I had three hands, the usual two being occupied with *your* mess."

"But you make such a lovely job of things, Orlando. You're so diligent in all that you do. Everything."

There had been a certain emphasis and inflexion in the last remark that made Coppersmith look up at his friend and catch the glint in his eye. "Don't know what you mean," he mumbled and turned red.

"I shan't enlighten you; no risqué talk before dinner. And I wonder what they'll give us at high table? Have a bit of a hankering for duck."

"Glad that you've got your appetite back, Jonty," one boot finished, the other about to be attacked with brush and cloth, "I was a great deal worried about you yesterday."

Stewart started to swing in his chair, a nervous habit that Coppersmith had noticed him employ before on the rare occasion when he was unsettled. "Do you know, I was so happy after I came back to St. Bride's, Orlando. I had been full of concern, there were so many memories here, bad and good, but from the very first night I was content. You made me feel content."

Their eyes met, they both smiled and Stewart continued. "I hoped that I would find more happiness with you than I've ever known and I do believe that's still possible, were it not for this maniac." He slammed the legs of his chair down. "We could be so content together Orlando, if this shadow didn't hang over us. Such a night we had on Saturday, such a night, but I don't feel that we can do it again until the murderer is found. I don't feel safe now, not at all."

"Then you should lock your bloody door, Jonty, anyone could have walked in here, you know." Orlando slammed the boot and brush down on the table to emphasize the point.

Stewart looked sheepish. "I know. I'm an idiot, really, it's just force of habit. That's probably what the 'lurker', or whoever the murderer is, relies on. We're all careful for a while and then we slip again—I bet that Marchbanks had stopped locking his door, too. But then even a firmly secured door won't stop someone entering if the person inside the room trusts them and lets them in."

Lessons in Love

Coppersmith stopped buffing and felt completely stunned, this astounding and simple fact really sinking in for the first time. "That's true, isn't it? If the maniac is so seemingly innocent and above suspicion, he could knock and be let in anywhere."

"Of course it's true, Orlando. That's what makes it so depressing; you could eventually find yourself mistrusting everyone."

"A healthy dose of mistrust on your part wouldn't come amiss." Orlando frowned. "And have you had any further success with your Monday afternoon group?"

Stewart looked up with an unusually serious expression on his handsome face. "They'd shut up like clams today, Orlando. No willingness to gossip from any of them, all except little Johnson-Browne who chattered on happily about the badge and the fact that the police had been to see him about it and were working their way around all the lunch party. Something has badly spooked the other three. Mackenzie looked as white as a sheet and Trumper could hardly make a sensible comment at all about Othello." He pondered for a moment, turning a now immaculate rugby boot over in his hands. "I think I need to talk to Jackson, see if he noticed anything at that luncheon. Will you talk to your crowd tomorrow?"

"I think not. I suspect that Ferguson knows more than he's telling but short of putting him on the rack I can't see how one extracts the information." He glanced at Stewart out of the corner of his eye. "Will you come to my rooms this evening after hall? We could say that we were playing chess."

"I will not, Orlando, not tonight." Jonty seemed to take an inordinate interest in his rugby boot.

"But why? I got the cold shoulder yesterday as well. Don't you desire me now that you've been with me?"

Stewart looked up, indignation written in his eyes. "Did you get that stupid line out of one of those wretched books, Orlando? The desperate victim to the cunning seducer?"

111

"I wish you wouldn't mention those books, I was an idiot about them."

"Yes, you were." Stewart appeared to regain his calm. "You must know that I do still desire you—I always will, I hope—but this third murder has made me incredibly depressed and I don't think it safe to sleep together again for the moment. Please trust me when I say that all I want to do at present is curl up in my own bed, alone, and try to clear my mind. By the time Wednesday comes I hope to have the will again to beat the living daylights out of some poor History don." He must have seen how horrified Coppersmith was and began to laugh. "The rugby, Orlando. I'm not proposing committing grievous bodily harm in the SCR. Talking of which, I can feel my stomach rumbling, perhaps there is still hope, after all." He flung the boot down and they got ready for the delights of high table.

Tuesday proved a long day, hard work for both of the fellows, with Coppersmith having a particularly trying time with his supervision group. Far from clamming up, they proved most voluble in giving their opinions on the murders, even Valentine making serious suggestions this time, but as far as Coppersmith could see, all the contributions were totally worthless. St. Bride's was full of ridiculous theories that were no doubt making it easier for the killer by muddying the waters of fact.

Jonty went to see Jackson, as he'd proposed, on the pretext of borrowing an interesting book that Jackson had once offered to lend him. Stewart had, of course, never an intention of reading about squids or cicadas or whatever tosh was in the thing, but he'd filed away the offer in case it should ever prove useful. As it did now.

Jackson opened the door to his room very gingerly; he at least was showing every sign of caution. He listened to Jonty's request, beamed with pleasure and gleefully produced the book in question, a weighty tome which

Stewart took with as much enthusiasm as if it had been an original letter from Richard Burbage.

Jonty produced his most charming smile. "Bit of a rumpus after your lunch party. All that fuss about a little badge." He didn't admit that he'd been the one to bring the object to the police's notice. That would only have complicated matters.

"They've been asking us all about it." Jackson was almost bouncing with the excitement that being so close to *an important clue* must have generated in him. To Jonty's eyes he appeared to be no more than a boy, but then all the victims had been so young, if not innocent. And it was likely that the killer was the same.

"I don't suppose that there was much that you could tell them."

"No, I hadn't seen the thing at all until they showed it to me. But I wouldn't have done at the time, it was such a busy party, sir—very lively! Ingleby arrived in the foulest temper, so Mackenzie saved the day by starting some of his sleight of hand tricks. What a hit he was." Jackson grinned, and began to relate some of the illusions the man had produced.

"Amateur magician, is he?"

"Oh, yes, and a very talented one. Makes us all amazed with his feats. Even Trumper stopped rushing about with bottles and plates for five minutes to watch the fun." His expression changed. "I'm a bit worried about old Trumper, Dr. Stewart. This business has got him pretty low, I've never seen him so unlike his usual self. The sooner this maniac is caught, the better for all of us."

Stewart wondered how many people in the college were saying exactly the same. He thanked Jackson for the book and made his way over to the police station to report on this interesting conversation. He was met by Cohen, Inspector Wilson having gone to Durham. The police had been informed of a series of similar crimes occurring at the University there a year previously, the basic elements—

strangulation, the notes, the open window—being the same. The culprit hadn't been brought to book, although most suspected one of the very minor royals and the whole thing had been effectively hushed up.

Wilson wasn't just seeking for links between the two cases, he was engaged to talk to an eminent professor who had views upon the significance of the window. The jovial sergeant informed Dr. Stewart that these theories varied from deep and psychologically significant to the simple need to get in fresh air to clear the culprit's body odor. And with a dramatic roll of his eyes he showed Jonty exactly what he thought of high-blown ideas.

Orlando knew that he shouldn't have come to watch the rugby. He should have gone to the dentist and had his teeth pulled out, it would have been less painful. It wasn't as if the game was bad, it was a very exciting match, good end-to-end stuff and plenty of points scored. It wasn't bad weather, it was much milder than it had been the last month and the sun was high enough in the sky to have the suggestion of heat about it. The problem was the bloody stupid way that Jonty Stewart threw himself headlong into every tackle. Bodies crunching together, stomach-churning sounds of bone and muscle in collision—that was what was so very distressing. And Jonty always seemed to emerge from the melee with a daft grin and, usually, the ball.

Orlando died a thousand deaths watching him. *If the idiot ends up in hospital, I'll never forgive him; he has no right to put me through this.* At one point a particularly large and nasty history don grabbed Stewart by the back of his shirt, swung him round and deposited him in a heap. Coppersmith had to pace up and down to restrain himself from going and laying the man out there and then. His attention was soon grabbed by whoops of joy and the clapping of backs. Jonty had scored a try and Orlando had missed it, too bound up in his anger to watch. *And now he'll never forgive me.*

Eighty minutes had never taken so long to pass, but pass they eventually did and Coppersmith raised the strength to applaud first the losers (a despondent but gracious School of History) and then the winners (a jubilant but sporting School of English) off the pitch. Stewart, muddy and ragged but gloriously happy, bounced up to him. "Did you see, Orlando? I scored a try, the first for nearly nine months."

"It was wonderful, Jonty," Coppersmith lied, but there was no way he was going to admit the awful truth. "You had a cracking game."

"Not bad at all. Think I'll have a bruise or two come morning, but each of them will be worth it, even the one on my backside where that brute dumped me on it. Got my revenge, though." He pointed to the man's bloody face with a gleeful grin. "Raked him with my studs."

Coppersmith was horrified. "How could you do that, Jonty? And then shake his hand afterwards?"

Stewart huffed. "Are you telling me, in all your years of playing rugby, that you never raked someone or thumped them when nobody was looking? Because if you are, I simply won't believe you. Not even you could be so innocent."

Orlando felt mortally offended, though whether at the implication of dirty play or the comment on his naivety, he couldn't tell. Jonty had overstepped the mark and had to pay for it, so Coppersmith simply turned on his heels and stomped off, leaving Jonty to stare after him.

Wednesday evening before high table and Coppersmith wasn't in his usual chair. He slunk into hall just before the grace, avoiding Stewart's eye and not speaking to anyone. The two men had deliberately avoided each other since the end of the rugby match and, if truth be known, they'd never really fallen out this badly before. They simply had no idea how to effect reconciliation.

Leaving hall, they were both struck by the same thoughts. *We have to sit together. If we're seen not to, it'll raise such a fuss. Perhaps he'll go back to his rooms; if not, I'll go to mine.* Rescue came in the form of Lumley, the chaplain, who linked his arm through Stewart's, swept the man up and led him off to the far recesses of the SCR where he wanted to discuss some rather bold plans he had for the Ash Wednesday service. Jonty was one of the few fellows who really believed the words he spoke when they got to the Creed and Lumley valued his opinion, which was always honestly given, if a little constrained this night.

Stewart's concentration wandered from the desirability of changing the order of service to the desirability of reaching a settlement with his friend. He surreptitiously risked a glance in the direction of their chairs and was astonished. Dr. Coppersmith was sitting in *his* seat. In *Jonty Stewart's* seat, the cheeky bugger. Suddenly stating the conviction that whatever changes the chaplain wanted to make would be absolutely the right ones, Jonty bowed his head to Lumley and made his way across to Orlando.

The man looked deadly serious, as stern as he'd been that first night they met, but this time *his* backside was in the wrong place and Stewart had the distinct feeling it had been put there to deliberately provoke him to action. The ploy had succeeded.

"That is my chair, sir."

Dr. Coppersmith looked up to see the piercing blue eyes that always melted his stony heart gazing down at him. "I do apologize, sir. I've had a trying day and I've forgotten some of our customs. I hope that you'll forgive me." He bowed slightly.

"Well, Coppersmith, we are great ones for resisting change and the particular chair a man inhabits after high table is regarded as sacrosanct." Jonty indicated the empty seat next to him. "This place doesn't seem to be occupied;

Lessons in Love

perhaps you might like to use it?"

They sat down in their rightful places and tried hard not to smile. Stewart lost the battle in very short time. "Coppersmith, you are such an ass. When I saw you were sitting in my chair, I knew exactly what you were doing. Didn't have the guts to say *sorry I stormed off today Dr. Stewart* and had to break the ice somehow."

"There really are times when I feel like punching you. This is one of them, but you will note that I'm restraining my fists. I went through all sorts of horrors watching you playing this afternoon—do you know that you crunched into a tackle or some such foolery once every minute and twenty-seven seconds? I worked it out. And every time I was convinced that you wouldn't get up again and that I'd have to take you to the hospital with a broken leg or worse." Orlando didn't just feel angry, he was beside himself with distress. "And I didn't even see you score your try because I was so upset at that chap dumping you on the ground that I couldn't bear to look any more."

"You missed my try? Then why on earth did you lie to me about it?"

"Because I couldn't bring myself to admit that I'd been such an idiot. And then for you to say that you'd deliberately trodden on that same chap's face. It's hardly sporting."

Jonty tossed his head. "Oh, Dr. Coppersmith, it was part of the game, just like sharing a pint or two of beer with the same fellow afterwards, which I did, incidentally, and you missed out on a noble brew by not coming with us."

"You went and drank with him? After what you'd done to his cheek?"

"But of course I did. There were no hard feelings between us, so I don't see what you're so upset about."

"I'm upset because you seem to take no care of yourself. You're still two weeks shy of the time the doctor said you could play, you were totally reckless on the field today, and you're still not locking your door at night."

Orlando stopped abruptly, he hadn't meant to say the last part. Now the cat was well and truly out of the bag.

"How on earth do you know that I don't lock my door every night?"

Coppersmith took a deep breath, decided he couldn't lie, and continued sheepishly. "Because I check."

"You check?" Stewart's eyebrows were disappearing into his hairline. "You come and test my door? Is this every night?"

"The last two. Since I found the door unlocked that day you made me clean your filthy boots."

Jonty began to laugh, a great rumbling laugh that wouldn't be stopped. He eventually wiped his eyes and continued. "Oh, Dr. Coppersmith, I can just imagine you creeping around in the dead of night making sure that I'm alright. I'm most deeply touched." He laid his hand on Orlando's arm, just very briefly, and smiled the most loving of smiles.

Coppersmith could feel himself coloring and began to murmur incoherently about *not sleeping well, needing the fresh air, no trouble at all to just come along a few staircases and check the door.*

Jonty looked at him long and hard before leaning over and saying in a voice that was loud enough for anyone close by to hear, "Shall we repair to your rooms for that game of chess, Dr. Coppersmith?"

Orlando looked up, caught a distinctly fevered look in his friend's eye and nodded. It was what he'd been fervently hoping for over the last few days, another invitation to share their passion, and he wasn't going to turn it down. They finished their coffees, left the SCR and wandered across to Coppersmith's set without another word spoken.

They often did play chess, or whist, which Coppersmith preferred. But this night the board was left unset and the cards undealt. They stared into the fire, which was newly sprung into life under the persuasion of the poker, and held hands. Slowly, Stewart snuggled closer to his friend, laying his head on Orlando's shoulder. "I can't stand being miserable any longer—you matter too much to me to keep denying ourselves. Is there any chance that you would want me to stay tonight?"

"Please." Coppersmith paused for reflection. "I'd want you to stay every night, although I don't suppose that's possible. So that I could keep you safe."

"Just a little awkward, Orlando. It would make things a bit obvious." Stewart smiled and kissed Coppersmith on the brow. "Just need to, you know..." he indicated the bathroom with a movement of his head. "Won't be a moment."

When he emerged from the toilet, Jonty found that his friend had already entered the bedroom and was stripping off his clothes, so he began to do likewise, starting with his shoes and socks, about which he was probably developing a complex. He was getting to grips with his shirt when strong, naked arms enfolded him. Orlando was now stripped and had pressed close to his friend's back.

"You saved my life, Jonty." The words were merely breathed into his ear.

"I never did, Orlando. I sometimes don't understand you at all." Stewart placed his hands on Coppersmith's arms, caressing the smooth skin and producing all sorts of tingling sensations.

"But you did, you know. If you'd not come along and sat in my chair I quite likely wouldn't have got around to kissing anyone, despite what I said in the Fellows' Garden. And I certainly would never have done what we've done this past week. I'd have ended up an old shriveled misanthrope, interested in nothing but numbers and the honor of the college. How I would ever have coped with the knowledge of murders affecting St. Bride's, I shudder to think." He squeezed Stewart as tightly as he could manage without actually hurting him. "Bed, Jonty. Now?"

Stewart turned and stared in amazement. "I beg your pardon?"

Orlando felt rather pleased at having discovered such a dominant streak within himself; he was sure it was connected to making love to Stewart. He'd speculated several times about what would have happened if he'd discovered the delights of the flesh at an earlier age, like other men were supposed to, but had decided it was pointless to wonder. If it hadn't been with Jonty it wouldn't have counted, anyway. Nothing counted without him. "Bed, Jonty. Both of us, now?" He paused slightly in case he'd been too dominating. "Am I supposed to say please?"

"Idiot." Jonty kissed him. "Insatiable idiot." He kissed him again, with more passion. "Magnificent, insatiable idiot." Jonty pulled at the buttons of Orlando's trousers. "Beautiful, magnificent, insatiable idiot." He pulled roughly at the tail of Coppersmith's shirt. "Wonderful, beautiful…"

"Oh, do shut up." Orlando had been putting a lot of thought into this. He'd taken all the lessons of Saturday, remembered, considered and come to the conclusion he could improve upon them. All he needed was the chance to try and if Jonty didn't stop blethering, he'd never get it. When Coppersmith applied his mind to something mathematical, the results were truly startling, and he was hoping to use the same talent in his bed. He was going to make this so good, so astoundingly good, that Stewart would never consider even looking at anyone else. Or think about trying some of the racier stuff that was in Morcar's books. Orlando wasn't ready to be putting his talents to that just yet. He took Jonty's hand and drew him into the bedroom.

The narrowness of the little college bed wasn't a constraint; it forced their bodies together and they could legitimately enjoy every moment of proximity. Orlando doubted that his parents had ever known such physical closeness, layers of cotton and flannel and half the width of a double bed would have usually separated them, he guessed. And there would have been no question of them ever seeing their spouse in a state of even mild undress.

Such things weren't done in the Coppersmith household, as they weren't done in many a house in Victorian England. But now Orlando had held Stewart stripped and brazen in his arms and there was no secrecy between them. He knew where the little scars were on Jonty's shoulder, the marks he'd got falling out of a tree as a lad. And no doubt Stewart knew off by heart where all the moles were on Orlando's chest.

As Coppersmith gently pressed his friend onto the mattress, he shuddered slightly, thinking of what his mother would have made of him sprawling naked and shameless, becoming increasingly tousled from his encounter and beginning to take up the scents of sweat and of Jonty Stewart. He contemplated all that had happened these last twelve hours and for them to have gone from daggers drawn to the ultimate compliance amazed him. But then life continually amazed Orlando at present, in a way that it hadn't done these last twenty seven years. And the catalyst in it all had been Jonty Stewart, the man who was at that moment kissing him fiercely and whose hands were roving around, causing all sorts of incredible sensations.

It was going to take longer, much longer, to reach a climax this time. Orlando wanted the bliss to last until it got to the point neither he nor Jonty could stand it any longer. It was going to require a great deal of self control, as part of him just wanted to get to the crux as soon as possible.

"Will you stop thinking?" Stewart stopped kissing, stopped stroking, looked like he might either have a fit of giggling or smack Orlando one. "We're here, stark naked, in a lovely soft bed and in a state where the most amazing things are liable to happen at any moment and your brain's whirring like a blessed clockwork toy. For goodness sake, this isn't a tutorial."

Orlando didn't even bother to say he was sorry. He stopped thinking and began being amorous, properly amorous, finding all sorts of parts of Jonty's body to kiss and make the man groan in the process. He loved the way that Stewart's skin tasted, how it was soft in places and as rough as sandpaper in others. The sensation of Stewart's fingers on his own skin amazed him, how they seemed to instinctively know how long to stay and caress, when to move on and delight some other part of Coppersmith's flesh. And it was wonderful when Jonty crooned to him, murmuring words of love and subtly suggesting whether they might like to *try this just now as it would be rather nice, don't you think?*

When the natural end to it all came, Orlando was convinced that he couldn't have lasted another minute of such gratification without screaming or something equally embarrassing to be doing in a small college room. He'd been petrified that if he'd called out, someone might have come along, thinking a fourth victim was being attacked, so he'd pressed his mouth to Jonty's head and restrained all the urges to squeal or shout. One day, when the murder and mayhem was done, they might find themselves in a place where he could let himself go. But not in St. Bride's, and not with a killer at large.

Jonty woke at five o'clock, hearing the comforting sounds of the college chimes ringing the hour in. Last night had been an experience much more satisfying than anything Jonty had so far done with Coppersmith and, indeed, most of the things he'd done with Richard, who was neither the most innovative nor considerate of lovers. Stewart would be entirely satisfied to make love to this one man for the rest of his life—soul mates, bed mates, at home in each other's arms.

He carefully slipped from the bed, taking infinite care not to wake his friend, whose dark curls lay tousled on the pillow and who appeared ridiculously alluring in the thin ray of moonlight that penetrated the room. Dressing quietly, he placed a gentle kiss on Orlando's brow and departed, using the spare key to ensure that the door was securely locked behind him. Barely a noise he made as he went down the stairs and around the court. Thankfully not another soul was to be seen or heard all the way back to his own rooms.

But *he* was seen and heard. If he'd had eyes in the back of his head, like his mother seemed to have, he might have seen the skulking figure watching him leave Coppersmith's staircase. And the sight might just have made his flesh, still warm with the memory of Coppersmith's body, turn to ice.

Chapter Ten

Orlando lay in bed fingering the creases on the pillow left by his lover's head and pondering. He knew that he thought too much, Jonty told him the fact often enough, but he couldn't stop himself. It was as much a part of his nature as a cheeky grin was of Stewart's. His small bed felt curiously large and empty now that his friend had departed, and there wasn't even the merest bit of warmth remaining where his body had lain.

Coppersmith turned over again in his mind all the wonderful things which Jonty had introduced him to over the last few months and how his life had now changed beyond all perception. He was loved, he loved in return and now he'd been allowed to share the most precious of gifts. It wasn't just the act of love (as he was now brave enough to refer to it in his brain, although the words couldn't pass his lips) that had been such a revelation. It had been the extraordinary intimacy that preceded and followed. They could lie together in each other's arms, content in their devotion and at peace with each other and the world.

He thought about Stewart's chest, which had been his pillow for much of the night. He contemplated how much

Lessons in Love

he adored the prominent collarbones, the notch between them, how easy it was to kiss along the ridges and make Jonty giggle and moan and giggle again. And a few weeks ago Coppersmith had never so much as held another person's hand. He thought of years that they could spend together, of all the wonderful things that they could share in, or might share in once the threat was ended, once the maniac was caught. Back his thoughts came to the murders. Life at St. Bride's now was as stagnant as the water that had flooded the Backs and lay festering on the grass, unable to drain away. Until the shadow was lifted, the college couldn't function and he couldn't function either.

He felt sure that if he just took the facts, sorted them and applied his brain, a solution would become apparent. He also felt ashamedly arrogant to think that *he* could succeed where Wilson and Cohen hadn't so far, but he was driven to try. Impelled by the thought of Jonty Stewart naked, sleeping peacefully in his arms like a newborn babe, downy hair on the nape of his neck gently rising and falling under Coppersmith's breath. He wanted Jonty by his side every night, in a double bed preferably, with clean linen sheets and thick blankets.

What he got was Jonty Stewart banging on the door as if his life depended on it, waking half the staircase and dragging him from his pleasant daydreams into a cold dressing gown. "Morning, slug-a-bed," Stewart grinned as the door was opened. "Get that fire going, I'm absolutely perished here."

Orlando began to fumble with matches and firelighters, until Jonty took pity on him, pushed him out of the way and set to himself. "Why hasn't your bedder got this set up?"

"Told them I didn't want to be bothered in the morning anymore. Said they could come in later." Coppersmith turned red and studied his feet. "Didn't want to risk you being caught here with me."

"Big, gormless ass." Stewart kissed him gently on the forehead and sent him off to shave and dress while he made some coffee and toast. "Got a surprise for you when you're presentable," he yelled from the kitchen, causing Coppersmith to nick his face, as he was exceedingly wary now of any surprise that Jonty might care to give him.

Orlando emerged neat and tidy as ever apart from the slight cut to his face, and that having now been addressed with a styptic pencil. He wore the rather daring tie that Stewart had given him for Christmas, a tie that had rarely seen the light of day but was being brought out to demonstrate his gratitude for the night before.

Jonty poured the coffee, smeared the toast with butter and jam, and the two fellows plonked themselves on the settee and enjoyed the by now thriving blaze. "How does a day in London appeal to you, Orlando?" Stewart had made short work of his first piece of toast and was scoffing the second with gusto, spreading crumbs everywhere as usual.

"That would be very pleasant, Jonty. When and what are you proposing?" Coppersmith entertained no great hopes that Stewart might be proposing *next month, a trip round the museums.*

"This Saturday, Orlando, and to the theatre. There's a particularly fine production of Hamlet on at present, so I telegraphed my mother to get us tickets. She has it all organized, naturally, including booking us a table for luncheon. Just received a telegram to confirm it." He waggled the piece of paper at his friend who was amazed to see the length, and therefore the cost, of this communication.

"Hamlet? We're to see Hamlet?" Coppersmith didn't ask in an exasperated way, as he often did when a new thing was ventured, but in an intrigued and excited manner. He was named after a Shakespearean character, it had been one of the first things he'd ever confided to his friend, but he'd never been lucky enough to see a professional production of one of the Bard's plays. And now he'd have the opportunity to fulfill one of his life's ambitions

"Hamlet it is, then. And the best box in the house, or so

Lessons in Love

the lady at the theatre assured my mother," Jonty waved the telegram again, "and we'll be home in time for a little light supper somewhere."

London, lunch at the Savoy and a matinee at the Theatre Royal, back again on the train and cabs everywhere, Stewart being always flush with money. The prospect was enticing for both of them, but especially for Orlando who had little experience of the big city except for visits to other seats of learning. For him, Saturday couldn't come quickly enough. "I don't think I shall be able to concentrate on my lecture today, Jonty. I shall probably start rambling about madmen and dead fathers." He abruptly stopped, causing Stewart to look at him very closely.

"Are you alright? You look as if you were the one who had seen the king's ghost."

"Association of ideas, Jonty, that's all. Made me think of what's been going on here." It was a lie, Stewart must have known it was a lie and Orlando knew that Stewart must have known it was a lie, but neither man was going to go probing for or revealing the truth at this point. "Anyway, assuming that I get through these lectures and make some sense to the dunderheads, will I see you for a sherry here before hall?" If truth be known Coppersmith was actually making more sense than ever before to his lecture students, partly because he was addressing the back of the hall, rather than his shoes or his waistcoat. But taking sherry with his lover he would not be.

"Sorry, Orlando, there's an English meeting at St. Thomas' buttery tonight. Bit of a special 'do' to celebrate the Professor's birthday."

Coppersmith frowned. "That's so unfair. You were drinking with your mates yesterday, after the rugby match. Don't I get to see you at all tonight?"

Stewart eyed his friend closely again. His face had become pale and his blue eyes as cold as tempered steel. "You've had plenty of my company these last few weeks, Orlando. Aren't I allowed to have some time with my other

127

friends?"

Coppersmith desperately wanted to say *No, you're mine alone and I'll let no other take you from me* but he bit his lip and said nothing.

"I'm waiting for an answer, Orlando and I won't let up until I'm given it. Am I to spend all my time with you? Is that what you want of me?"

Coppersmith slowly shook his head. "No, not at all. I want us to be together as much as possible, but I can't monopolize you. That would be very wrong."

Jonty gently lifted up his friend's head and regarded him. "You need to find some interests of your own, Orlando. You can't go back to just sitting in that chair on your own when I'm not around. You're a different person now and don't shake your head, *you are* and you know it. You've outgrown the confines of the SCR, of this college. There's a whole world out there that we can explore together but it won't be possible unless you're ready to step out on your own as well. Find a chess club, or join in with the card school which I'm told goes on down at St. Thomas'. Risk your Achilles tendon and take up rugby again, or go to the winter cricket nets. Do something that's not led by me. Amaze me, Orlando!"

Coppersmith nodded slowly this time. "I'll think on what you've said, Jonty, I promise. But I don't think you have the first idea of how difficult some of those things would be for me now, I've become so set in my ways..."

"Nonsense! You showed no sign of being set in your ways last night, and don't blush, because there was no shame in evidence then. Show half the bravado at the Thomas' card school that you showed in your bed and you'll put them all to shame." Stewart rose, spilling crumbs everywhere. "Now I have a lecture to give, too, and it will be one of my finest, I think. The sonnets. Such meat to get into there, Orlando and fresh inspiration provided in this very room, no, I correct myself, in *that* very room," he gave a tip of his head towards the bedroom, "last night." Stewart

Lessons in Love

spied a stray boiled sweet on the table, stuffed it in his mouth and left the room, whistling as contentedly as any man could be in that benighted college.

The rest of Thursday passed slowly, too slowly for Orlando's liking. It wasn't just the anticipation of their weekend trip that made the time drag, like the days before Christmas for a little boy; it was the talking to he had received from Jonty. *He wants me to find an interest outside St. Bride's, outside of us.* The thought unnerved him greatly. He'd rarely sought any activity outside the college these last six years and without Stewart to metaphorically hold his hand he was quite simply frightened. But he would have to do it, of course, Jonty wouldn't let the subject drop and he couldn't risk disappointing his lover, the man had made that quite clear.

Every time this disturbing thought cropped up, Orlando diverted it by thinking on the murders again. He could argue with Stewart that helping the police took preference over his social life at any point, but he was deceiving himself again, he knew. They *had* helped Inspector Wilson, but they all seemed to be no further on. Cohen had deferred questioning Mackenzie about his sleight of hand skills until his superior returned from the scene of the other crimes—this Orlando knew because he'd met the man in the market place and been given not just an update but a promise of further information should anything have turned up in Durham.

Coppersmith dined quietly at high table and took his lonely place in the SCR, trying very hard not to eye the empty seat beside him and failing miserably. He didn't want to feel jealous but he couldn't help it. As far as he was concerned, Jonty Stewart was his, his alone and the rest of the world could go hang before they got their greedy hands on him.

Lumley spied what was happening, took pity on the young man and came over to chat. He very pointedly drew an unused chair over to the other side of Coppersmith's, so as not to invade the sacred and empty spot. "Dr. Stewart with his other colleagues tonight, I presume? Our common room always seems as if several of the lights have been put out without his presence to brighten proceedings."

Orlando could hardly bear to reply, the chaplain having come so close to his own feelings. "Aye, it is. He always has a laugh and a joke to share. And all of them entirely suitable for genteel company," he added hastily.

"I never doubted that for a moment," the chaplain grinned. "But all the same he doesn't seem in the highest of spirits at present. He looked as close to sad yesterday as I've ever seen him. Is this business getting him down very much?"

Coppersmith was torn between seeking sympathy and help for Jonty from the man who was probably closest to him in the college, after himself, and keeping Stewart's state of mind close confined, being entirely able to deal with it on his own. Fortunately he was saved the dilemma of decision by Lumley's resuming.

"And you look tired yourself, Dr. Coppersmith. I believe that you're helping the police as much as you can, but that will be an onerous task on top of your college duties. You must not overstretch yourself."

Orlando knew exactly why he appeared tired but he was definitely *not* going to share that knowledge with the chaplain. "I won't, Dr. Lumley, and I'll endeavor to advise Dr. Stewart the same. Whether he'll take my advice is another matter, as you know." He ventured a little smile and took his leave with as much dignity and grace as he could muster.

Friday morning, Coppersmith found in his pigeonhole a paper bag containing six ounces of bulls-eyes and a little note that simply stated *Idiot xxx*. Whether this was an apology or reprimand he neither knew nor cared, but he carefully placed the slip of paper in his wallet with one or two other little notes that Stewart had left him in the past.

So Friday began very well and continued to get better. The sun shone gloriously out of a penetratingly blue sky, several of Orlando's thesis students started to show glimpses of truly original thinking and one of his fellow dons invited him to join a bridge four at St. Francis' College, time and date to be arranged but very soon. Jonty Stewart wouldn't dare complain now. He, Orlando Coppersmith, had organized his very own entertainment and while he felt slightly daunted at an actual date and time appearing in his pigeonhole, he wasn't going to admit it to his friend.

He didn't see Stewart until late afternoon, when they met at Inspector Wilson's request in the Police Station. The man had made some interesting discoveries in Durham, he explained in his summoning note, which he wanted to share with them. Interesting they certainly were, but not those concerning the window. Poor Wilson had been made to listen to an hour and a half of theories about the opening (and shutting) of casements, all of which might prove interesting in retrospect once the man had been caught, but none of which seemed to advance the cause of his pursuers.

What he'd learned about the similar case, however, had proved very relevant, for at least three people at St. Bride's had links to the college involved. Ferguson had attended for interview at the time one of the murders had occurred, Trumper had a brother at the University and Mackenzie's cousin was one of the lecturers in physics. No other links had been identified, albeit that wasn't to say that they didn't exist, but it was interesting to find the case turning time and again to this small group of students.

No one was suggesting for a moment that any of these young men had been the murderer in Durham, the authorities there being fairly certain that the culprit had been identified and, though unlikely to ever stand trial, he was now locked away in a genteel 'nursing home' where he couldn't cause further harm. The possibility was that one of the St. Bride's students had found out about the killings and had, for whatever his own ends turned out to be, decided to copy them.

Orlando considered a moment, then asked, "And did they ever ascertain why these killings occurred, or was the man in question just a lunatic?"

"As I understand it, Dr. Coppersmith, there had been some unpleasantness in his childhood at the hands of an elderly male relative." Wilson's audience looked expectantly but no more detail was forthcoming. "It had quite turned his brain, although he appeared relatively normal on the outside. Revenge on the type, I guess."

Stewart had become paler and quieter as the discussion proceeded, unable to manage more than one biscuit with his tea. "I'm not clear," he ventured, "why you are choosing to share this with us. Will you be telling the Master, too?"

Wilson and Cohen exchanged glances. "No," the senior officer eventually replied, "I don't think that we'll burden Dr. Peters further until we've more than just suspicions to go on. We've decided to tell you because we don't want you to put yourselves further at risk. Things got very nasty in Durham towards the end. There were only three victims, like here so far, but the last case was particularly gruesome in terms of what had been done to the body afterwards. I only found this out when I talked to the officer who first attended the scene. The gory details had been very effectively hushed up otherwise." Wilson glanced again at Cohen and seemed to receive a faint nod of agreement. "And so I'm asking you to leave well alone where these three young men are concerned. We're extremely grateful for what you've already done, but it must be left to us now, I beg of you." Wilson eyed the two ashen men and must have thought that his message had sunk home. "I will keep you informed of what we find out. Especially after Mr. Mackenzie explains what he knows about that badge." They concluded with the usual civilities and the two fellows began their return to St. Bride's, shaken and rather angry.

"Why call us off now?" Coppersmith was looking more furious with every step he took further from the station and closer to his sanctuary. "The risk of strangulation has always been present—why worry about what might happen to a body afterwards? Why is it suddenly more dangerous?" A look of horror crossed his face. "Can they know about us?"

"I hope not, with all my heart." Jonty shuddered. "Perhaps it's simply because these three men with the connection to Durham are close to us, Dr. Coppersmith. We welcome them into our rooms, even though there are other people present, and we've been fairly free with our questioning of them and their friends. I think that it's all a little too *close* for the constabulary's comfort and I for one should be relieved that we've an excuse to put the sleuthing down with a clear conscience."

"Will you really be relieved?" Orlando stopped and looked closely at his dearest friend. "Tell me the absolute truth."

"Part of me certainly will be, the part that jumps every time there's a knock at my door." Stewart considered. "But I suspect I'd regret it eventually. I've rather enjoyed being Watson to your Holmes and the intellectual part of the proceedings, the weighing of evidence and forming of theories in my mind, has rather taken my mind off the intrinsic horror of it all." He smiled wistfully. "And I do wish that you could have been given the opportunity of solving the case and being a hero to the college."

Coppersmith laughed, a sound which Jonty hadn't expected to hear at that point. "Sherlock Holmes I think not, Dr. Stewart; I'm far too handsome and self-effacing. But I'd desperately like to be in on the chase for this, for St. Bride's sake if not for my own."

Jonty stopped, feeling rather conspiratorial all of a

sudden. "Don't have to take their advice, Dr. Coppersmith. We could act off our own backs, you know."

"Aye, we could that." The glint in Jonty's eye was mirrored. "As long as you give me your solemn word that you won't put yourself into danger."

Stewart put one hand on his heart and raised the other as if taking an oath in court. "I sincerely swear that I will keep myself safe and secure and well and pure and chaste and anything else that you require." He grinned. "Only I *won't* be available to fulfill any particular requirements tonight. Oh, don't look like I've taken your bull's-eyes back. If we're to spend all tomorrow in London, then I must earn my play by marking Mackenzie's and Trumper's work. And it'll earn me an awful lot of playing, I can assure you."

Coppersmith reluctantly nodded his agreement. "As long as you promise to spend some time in the SCR explaining Hamlet to me—I'm an idiot as far as the Bard's plots are concerned and I want to be well briefed for tomorrow."

"My pleasure. The same chairs as always." A very tender smile lit Jonty's face. "*Our* chairs…"

The train sped down into Hertfordshire, the wintry skies threatening some late snow that Saturday morning, but so far not producing it. Coppersmith loved trains; not that he traveled very often, but the sensation of racing past trees and fields delighted him and the glimpses of backs of houses and tiny cottage gardens piqued his imagination. He considered Jonty out of the corner of his eye, but the man was fighting the newspaper into something like submission and didn't notice. There were questions he desperately wanted to ask, but was afraid of spoiling the day. In the end he decided that the day would be ruined anyway if he couldn't clear his mind so he ventured, "Dr. Stewart, may I ask you something very personal?"

"Hm, I'm sorry? Something personal? Ask away—as

Lessons in Love

long as I'm not obliged to answer." A grin appeared. A very typical Stewart grin.

"Those boys at your school…"

The grin disappeared.

"…I'm sorry to distress you, believe me, but I need to know whether that awful experience left you feeling murderous towards them? Would you have killed them if you could?"

Jonty considered a long time before replying. "Probably at the time, if I could have got away with it. If I met them now, possibly, with the same proviso. Why do you want to know?"

"It occurred to me that the college murderer might have been subjected to something similar and would seek his revenge on any man who lay with another, their all being tarred with the same brush as far as he was concerned. He heard of the Durham case and decided he would do the same."

Stewart sighed and looked at the carriage ceiling. "Can't we leave this business behind even for one day, Dr. Coppersmith? Can't we enjoy ourselves and forget the worry?"

Orlando reached over and gently touched his friend's sleeve. "We will leave it behind, we'll enjoy ourselves, but I must have this answered now. Is this a common occurrence, in boarding schools, and could it have affected our man? Like the murderer at Durham was said to have been hurt as a lad?"

Jonty sighed again and gave his friend a look horribly tinged with coldness and anger. "It's all too common in any single sex society. It happens in the armed forces, too, I understand. I think it quite likely that our man's grudge could be based on something deep in his own heart; if he just hated all men who lay together I think that he'd have been more likely to simply report them to the police and let them face public disgrace. There's more to this than moral outrage, Dr. Coppersmith, much more." Stewart returned to his newspaper and refused to talk about the subject again that day.

The train slid into Liverpool Street station and Jonty positively bounced onto the platform. He loved the city, the bustle and smells, the noise and excitement. He was as happy eating pie and mash or jellied eels from some stall in the East End as he was taking Chateaubrian at the Savoy. But it was to the latter establishment that he took his lover and gave him free run of the menu, the only proviso being that Coppersmith didn't indulge so much that he fell asleep and snored through the show.

Orlando took a little clear soup, an excellent lobster salad and a selection of cheeses. Stewart stuffed his face with pate and fillet steak and treacle tart—much to his friend's amazement, given the advice he'd received—and they shared a bottle of hock. The doorman poured them into a cab and they arrived at the theatre in ample time to find their box. It was one with a surprisingly unrestricted view and in which they might just venture holding hands with no fear of discovery, should things became too dramatic onstage.

The production was wonderful, set and costumes being a monument to their art and the verse speaking as good as anyone could want. There were only one or two of the supporting cast who would have benefited by heeding Hamlet's advice to *not saw the air too much with your hand*, the rest being above reproach. At the end Coppersmith stood and clapped till his hands were sore, like an overgrown schoolboy after having watched his heart-throb perform. Jonty's eyes were welling with tears of joy and he had to gulp in huge amounts of air to overcome it.

They were soon in the train again, heading north this time and the light already gone. It was difficult to see anything outside because of the reflections from the lamp, but Orlando didn't mind, because his dearest love had fallen asleep at his side and no one could come and harm them here. He was far too excited to fall asleep himself, content instead to go back over the play in his mind.

Though this be madness, yet there is method in't. There was method in the St. Bride's murderer's madness, certainly. He couldn't be overtly insane or he would have been caught. He must at least appear normal most of the time—perhaps a Hamlet in reverse, feigning sanity. He'd kept things simple, leaving no clue to his identity and, whatever the reason he'd taken that badge in the first place, he'd subsequently planted it on someone else at Jackson's party. Orlando was convinced that he hadn't just dropped it idly after being so careful about everything else. Mackenzie had been at that party and so had Trumper; did the murderer know of their connection to Durham and try to forge a connection to one of them? Or had Mackenzie, with his magic tricks, been the one to plant the badge, using sleight of hand?

The lady doth protest too much, methinks. Marchbanks had protested too much and a fat lot of good it had done him. It had probably contributed to his death and he might have done better to keep his head down and say nothing. Someone understood what that boldness had really meant and had taken action. Or perhaps he'd already known about Marchbanks' inclinations, if the murderer was also this 'lurker in the night' who crept about spying. He would see who left whose room and when, he might even hear the unmistakable sounds of lovemaking behind locked doors. Perhaps he'd even seen Jonty leave Coppersmith's rooms.

This is miching mallecho; it means mischief. Mischief was being wrought in Orlando's college again and again, and he felt powerless. Powerless even to guarantee safety to the most precious thing he had ever known.

Into a towering passion. This was a crime of passion, he was sure. Coppersmith had at last learned what ardor really was and he'd begun to understand how it could drive a person to madness. He was certain the murderer was someone like him—an innocent—who'd been introduced against his will to acts of lust and desire. He couldn't have been as lucky as Orlando had, to have a tender and devoted friend to lead him into the unknown territory of sexual pleasure. Coppersmith was suddenly sure that this murderer had been abused and left broken, and it had eventually led the victim to take a course of the most desperate revenge. But something must have triggered him into action this year. Perhaps he'd heard about the case in Durham during the Christmas holidays and that had proved catalyst enough. Maybe something or somebody in St. Bride's itself had come along and changed his life, as Jonty had changed Orlando's. Forever and irrevocably.

Despite the fact that they were in a well lit, first class carriage of a busy train, Coppersmith slipped his hand inside Stewart's and held it tight until they were safely in their station.

Chapter Eleven

Sunday morning and the chaplain had taken as his text The Gospel according to Matthew, chapter eighteen, verse six: 'Whoso shall offend one of these little ones which believe in me', preaching a mighty sermon about the evils of sullying the innocent and hurting the weak. Coppersmith cast a glance along his shoulder—Stewart was ashen, head bowed and contemplating his hands which were tightly gripping his prayer book. Jonty usually enjoyed Lumley's sermons but this one was too close to home for comfort. Orlando indulged in his recurring *what I would do to those men from his school if I ever found them* fantasy, suddenly realized that the thought was not at all appropriate to the setting, felt guilty and began to look at the faces of the undergraduates instead.

Mackenzie looked pale and uncomfortable, too. Ingleby seemed troubled. Ferguson appeared thoughtful, as he so often did and Trumper looked as if he'd shut off to all the world and retreated within himself. Three of these men had a link to Durham and Coppersmith was convinced that the solution lay with them, but how could he ever bring it to the light?

On Sunday afternoon, Orlando found a note in his pigeonhole from Mattheson to say that the bridge game was set for the Monday evening at half past seven. It said that the players generally dug into sandwiches and snacks beforehand, provided by whoever was hosting on the evening, so that the range of times for hall which applied at the participants' colleges wouldn't hamper them. It also suggested that Orlando might like to call in to the SCR at St. Francis' that very afternoon at four o'clock to observe a game in progress and see the bidding system they used. He took the note straight around to Stewart's rooms and waved it in his face triumphantly.

"A bridge four? Down at St. Francis'? Well, you *have* amazed me, Orlando, well and truly." Stewart ruffled Coppersmith's dark hair affectionately and smiled. "Can you remember what it was like that first evening in the SCR? You wouldn't even tell me your surname, no you wouldn't, so don't look so incredulous. You were such a funny old thing, you know, and I think I was in love with you before the week was out. Had to bide my time, but I knew it would be worth it in the end. And now you're going out of the college and playing bridge. Splendid!" He beamed and looked gorgeous and Orlando wished that he hadn't been going to anywhere but his friend's bedroom.

"What will you do with yourself, Jonty?"

"I'll just spend the afternoon with The Two Gentlemen of Verona, Orlando. Not the most entertaining of companions, but I need to put some fresh thoughts about them to one of my graduate students on Wednesday so I want to get myself up to speed. On Tuesday I'll have yet another batch of work from the dunderheads to wade through. Now that brings us to Tuesday night and I have no idea what we could possibly do then." He cocked his head to one side—the *inquisitive little bird* look as Orlando thought of it—and smiled like a small boy trying to get some barley sugar from his nurse.

Coppersmith smirked. "Well, I can't think of anything either, Dr. Stewart, so unless you can clearly state an idea after high table that evening, I'll just have to snuggle up with Pythagoras in front of the fire." He raised an eyebrow, grinned again and scuttled off down the stairs, leaving Jonty speechless.

Orlando never made it to St. Francis' that afternoon. At three o'clock a knock came on his door and he tentatively opened it to find Mackenzie stammering and nervous on the threshold. "May I come in, Dr. Coppersmith?"

Orlando was reluctant; this went against all the rules he'd been drumming into Stewart about keeping safe. "What is it you want, Mackenzie?"

The lad looked down at his hands. They were writhing around each other like two snakes seeking for warmth. "I know that you've been helping the police, it's well known in the college. There's something I want to tell you, should tell Dr. Stewart really but don't want to worry him unnecessarily, because I may have got this wrong." He looked up, probably in an attempt to be appealing.

Coppersmith opened the door, let the young man in, then sat down at the big desk, keeping its bulk firmly between him and his visitor.

Mackenzie looked uncomfortable, eventually sat down, and began to talk. It was fairly unremarkable stuff, going back to the first murder and what he and the coterie of Stewart's Monday students had been doing and saying at the time. He carried on to the occasion of the second crime, giving chapter and verse about all their doings.

Orlando soon lost interest; he was hearing nothing new and his attention wandered into speculation and analysis. He observed Mackenzie's strong, nimble hands as they moved around while the student spoke. How easy it would be with hands like that to plant evidence on some hapless individual in the guise of a magic trick. How easy it would be with those hands to squeeze the life out of another person. How stupid *he* had been to let this man through the door. How hard it would be for anyone to know that there was anyone in this set of rooms with Coppersmith now, not even Jonty would miss him until it was far too late. He was supposed to be at St. Francis' and it would only be when Stewart found the seat next to him in the SCR unoccupied that he would be sought out and then Jonty would walk in here to find a dead body. Orlando shivered and tried to remain calm, willing his lover to think about him, to seek him out now.

Jonty's mind was at that moment not on Coppersmith, for once. He'd been dragged away from the company of the Two Gentlemen of Verona to help the hapless Trumper with his work on Othello.

The young man had come and pleaded for a moment of his tutor's time to discuss jealousy. "Because it's something that I just don't understand, Dr. Stewart. Revenge, like Hamlet, now I see that man's motivations entirely, but the Moor defeats me." He'd been ushered in, had laid a great sheaf of papers on Stewart's desk and looked confused.

Jonty tried patiently to explain for the umpteenth time the rationale behind the murder of Desdemona, but he could see that while Trumper could memorize what he was being told, learn it by rote to regurgitate in some test, he didn't understand the emotions involved and probably never would. It was going to be a long and weary afternoon.

Coppersmith's nerves were by now completely ragged. Was he sitting opposite a murderer, a cold blooded killer who was now calmly going through the history of his campaign of terror? Mackenzie had reached events surrounding the death of Marchbanks and Orlando felt he was witness to some rambling confession, although the

Lessons in Love

admission of guilt had yet to be made. He'd begun to think of things within easy reach that he might use to defend himself, when his attention was at last arrested.

"Which is when I realized that I had actually seen that badge being planted in Ingleby's pocket." Mackenzie had ended his tale as abruptly as he'd started it and was obviously awaiting a reaction.

"I beg your pardon, would you please explain the last piece again."

The student nodded, appearing puzzled; perhaps he'd heard tell of Coppersmith's formidable brain and was wondering why it did not seem to be in evidence today. "At the party that Jackson gave. Ingleby had hung his jacket up on the door and while I was doing my tricks I had seen someone fiddling with it, just out of the corner of my eye, and last night I woke up with the certainty that they'd been putting something into the pocket."

"Who was it then?"

"Trumper, sir. Only thing is I know he can't be the murderer because, as I said, he was with Jackson when Russell-Clarke was killed. Which is why I didn't go straight to the police."

Orlando leaped from his chair. "Well, young man, we shall go and find Mr. Trumper now and take him to the station ourselves if need be. Alibi or not, he has a question or two to answer."

Stewart had been going through sexual jealousy a third time when he noticed Trumper's hand fiddling with his papers. He looked on, horrified, as a cutthroat razor was produced from amongst them, a razor that was slowly brandished in front of him.

"I don't think that I'd have any chance of overpowering you, Dr. Stewart, you being much stronger and much more sensible than the others were. Can't use my bare hands, so I remembered hearing about someone using this." Trumper smiled simperingly, as if he were talking about a cake he'd brought to share for tea.

Jonty edged back on his chair, out of range of any knife thrust. "Are you really proposing to kill me?"

"It seems such a shame to do it, sir, but I really have no choice in the matter." The young man's face bore a steady, unworldly smile.

"But you do. We all have choices in terms of our actions, Mr. Trumper." Stewart could feel the beads of sweat beginning to form on his brow.

"You may call me by my name, sir. You'll be pleased to know that it comes from the Bard. I was christened Sebastian, although I'm rarely anything other than Trumper to most of the folks here. I'd be honored for you to address me by my proper name."

If Stewart had needed any further proof that he was in the presence of a very dangerous sort of insanity, then this was it. This lad was so exceedingly polite, so seemingly willing to please, despite having made it plain that he had every intention of killing the very person he was displaying such immaculate manners towards. "Well, Sebastian, if you truly believe something to be a shame, then don't indulge in it. It would do you much credit to resist."

"Oh, but I can't, Dr. Stewart, I'm obliged to have to carry this through. It's my solemn duty."

"And just why is that?" *If I can keep him talking I can gain time to think, or somebody might come along. Orlando will come.*

"Because men who lie with men deserve to die. They use little boys in the night and hurt them." Trumper became deathly pale.

A chink of light appeared in Jonty's brain. "Did they use you in the night, Sebastian? Is this why you hate them so much?"

"They did, sir. When I was at school, one of the masters used to visit me in the sick bay. I was a sickly child, often ill and frequently I had the place to myself. He used to say that

Lessons in Love

it was a special privilege, what he came and did, but I never found it so."

"I understand exactly what you say." Jonty felt that if he could engage the lad's attention, his sympathy, there was still a chance that the situation could be talked around. "At school I was visited in the night and used—by the older boys, not the masters. And it bloody well hurt and I felt desperately dirty and ashamed for years afterwards. I can commiserate with you on everything that happened." He smiled, hoping frantically to gain the lad's confidence.

"Oh, then you will understand exactly why I have to do it," Trumper beamed ecstatically and caressed the deadly blade. "I always knew that you would. You're so sympathetic, Dr. Stewart."

Coppersmith fairly sped around the court, walking as fast as his dignity would let him, following Mackenzie to Trumper's room. There was no reply, not for three sets of heavy raps on the door, so they set off for Jackson's staircase. The little lad opened the door gingerly but noticeably relaxed when he saw faces that he must have trusted. "Dr. Coppersmith, however can I help you?"

"We wondered if you knew where we could find Mr. Trumper." Orlando could barely contain the shaking in his voice, from utter terror at what the answer might prove to be.

"He was having trouble with his essay, sir so I suggested he go and ask Dr. Stewart for some advice."

Coppersmith stared, tried to speak but nothing came out, turned on his heels and ran, dragging Mackenzie with him.

"And is it your solemn duty to write those notes as well?" Stewart was determined to keep Trumper talking, while the lad sat and talked and merely fondled the razor there was hope. *Orlando would come.* Except, as he realized with a sickening feeling in the pit of his stomach, Orlando was at St. Francis' studying the delights of three no trumps and couldn't come. He was alone.

"Indeed, sir, one of the most important parts. That's why I was so cross when Jackson took away the one I left on Douglas'—Lord Morcar's—body. It had to be found and you were kind enough to make sure that the police were aware of it. I was sure that you would be the right person to go to." Trumper gave another simpering smile and Jonty felt chilled to the very bone. "I really should have killed Jackson, too, but that wasn't expected of me. Only the truly wicked, not the silly. My brother told me all about a similar case at his college up at Durham. Someone else was given a set of tasks to perform and when it became obvious to me that I had to do the same, I thought it might be appropriate to copy his methods. "

"And why did you go back to open the window? Was that in imitation of the other man?"

Trumper looked pleased. "Oh, you worked out that I went back, but then I always knew that you were clever, Dr. Stewart. Such expositions of the sonnets!" Jonty looked to see if the lad was being facetious, but he seemed to be in deadly earnest, merely continuing, "I had to open the window to let his soul go, sir."

Of course, so simple a superstition. Stewart remembered his old nurse telling him that this must always be done so that the spirit could depart from the corpse. And all the great minds had been going around in circles to work out a more meaningful explanation.

"You must have guessed by now that I saw you leave Dr. Coppersmith's rooms early on Thursday morning. It's taken me all this time to consider it, but I've decided that I'll kill you first as you'd be terribly upset were I to do anything to him. I've always been exceedingly fond of you, Dr. Stewart, more than fond, and I wouldn't like to see you suffer any sadness in the interim." The razor danced again

Lessons in Love

and Jonty began making calculations about whether he could simply apply all his weight in one lunge and wrest the thing from Trumper's hand. But the smallest determined stroke of the blade in the right place could prove deadly. Stewart knew very well that a cutthroat razor was a fearsome weapon.

"Tell me, sir, do you enjoy it when you make the beast with two backs?" Trumper cocked his head to one side, a movement that Jonty recognized as being habitually one of his own. He wondered whether this too was an imitation and couldn't work out whether the familiar motion, or the words that accompanied it, unsettled him most.

"Dr. Coppersmith and I have never made 'the beast with two backs', as you call it, Trumper, and I resent the accusation." It was true, he and Orlando had barely begun to explore the delights of the flesh—perhaps they never would now. "I stayed with Dr. Coppersmith because he was feeling unwell." It was a feeble effort, Jonty knew, but one that had to be tried.

Trumper smiled patronizingly. "I respect you enormously, Dr. Stewart, but you can't think that I'm going to believe that, can you?" He twirled the potentially lethal blade again and again.

Coppersmith ran as he'd never dared run through the courts of St. Bride's. Mackenzie flew in his wake, trying to understand what was going on.

"Go straight to the police and bring them here. Use the phone at the porters' lodge, anything, just get them here quickly." Orlando spoke without stopping.

"But why should Dr. Stewart be under such a threat as you think he is? Because of his sleuthing?"

"Indeed, Mr. Mackenzie, we've made ourselves too obvious in acting as Holmes and Watson, and I pray to God that we've not unleashed the terror upon ourselves." It was a reasonable explanation, it would suffice, but it wouldn't help Jonty one iota.

And Jonty was still fighting for his life. "You've too much confidence in my brains, Mr. Trumper. Some things still puzzle me. Did you take the badge when you returned to Morcar's rooms?"

"Oh no, Dr. Stewart, I'd already got that. I'd been admiring it very much while we were talking that evening. He came over and started to tell the whole story about the dining club and he was so trusting that it was easy just to reach around his neck. I think he may have thought that I was ready to kiss him, but I just squeezed with my hands like so." Trumper demonstrated with his wiry, nimble fingers. "Very easy, really." The explanation was totally matter of fact and he displayed no sense of guilt or embarrassment.

"Why should he think you were going to kiss him?" Stewart had begun to formulate a strategy of attack that would keep the blade away from his neck or chest, but he needed more time to prepare it.

"Because that's what he had to think, so that I could get close enough to strangle him. Get someone relaxed and they're easy prey."

Jonty felt like he was going to be sick. Sensations fluttered up and down his spine and crept up his neck. He breathed hard, trying to focus on staying calm and alert.

The boy continued. "I know I haven't got a handsome face, not like you, sir, but I can flatter well enough and undo the odd button here or there when it's needed. It's simple, really. All three of them just let me come into their rooms and talk and flirt and, well I don't need to tell you, Dr. Stewart. You know how it goes."

Jonty felt another chill traverse his spine, but he tried to keep the lad talking. And Trumper seemed willing enough to do it, for the moment. "The police seem to think that you have an unshakable alibi for the night of Russell-Clarke's

Lessons in Love

murder. You were with Jackson; he told me that you didn't leave."

The younger man laughed. "Now, Dr. Stewart, it was terribly easy to administer a little something in his lemonade. I got some powders from the doctor to help me sleep and I knew they'd be helpful sometime. He kept waking on and off and I just timed it to perfection; he was awake when I returned but I pretended I'd just been to the toilet. Easy. And now I really must get on with the job in hand, sir." Trumper rose from his seat, making Jonty force his limbs to do the same and they gradually moved across the room, Stewart desperately trying to keep both his distance and his eye on the blade.

They were concentrating so hard that neither of them heard the footsteps on the stairs and they were both stunned as the door flew open and Coppersmith burst into the room, instantly stopping as he saw the blade winking in the sunlight. The timing was unfortunate, Stewart's relief at seeing his friend making him lose his guard and Trumper closing the gap and grabbing him around the shoulders. Jonty couldn't make his superior strength count, his attacker raising the blade quickly and laying it flat against his throat.

"Don't come any closer, Dr. Coppersmith. I'm not afraid to do this."

"If you harm one hair on Dr. Stewart's head, I'll tear you limb from limb and I won't need a knife to help me. My bare hands will suffice." Orlando spoke quietly and calmly and it was all the more frightening for it. No one in the room doubted he was telling the truth.

"What pleasure will you get in revenge if Dr. Stewart isn't here to enjoy it with you?"

Orlando looked horribly distressed. Jonty was aware that whatever the young man knew already or had understood from the discussion in this room, he now comprehended the situation completely. There would be no pleasure in Coppersmith's life anymore if Stewart weren't there.

Orlando swallowed hard. "Then let me take Dr. Stewart's place. If you wish to take a life, take mine."

"I won't let you do that." Stewart was determined. "You won't sacrifice yourself for me, Orlando. It would be the ruin of two lives." Their eyes met and locked, all sorts of messages passing between them by looks alone.

Trumper's hand wavered and his grip lessened almost imperceptibly. Jonty thought that, for the first time since he'd started brandishing that razor, the lad seemed nervous. He'd no doubt expected Coppersmith's threats but the offer of the man's life as proxy seemed to have shocked him into inaction. Jonty felt the loosening of the arms that held him and acted, pushing his arms up and out so that he could fight loose. The razor flashed through the air, catching the ball of Stewart's thumb and making a great spurt of blood gush over the floor. Coppersmith's arm struck out across Trumper's body, causing the lad to let the blade go flying, the dreadful thing coming to rest under a chair.

Then Coppersmith was at Stewart's side in an instant, bringing out his handkerchief and tenderly applying it to the cut on his lover's hand. The two Fellows kept Trumper within sight all the time, anger vying with fear and concern for the mastery in their minds. The world had almost ended for them, not a minute ago, and now it was going to be all right, Jonty was going to be all right.

"I'm fine, Orlando, truly I am. It's just a superficial cut; I've suffered worse at rugby." Jonty managed a watery smile of reassurance, but he knew his face must be as pale as Orlando's was.

"I could never have forgiven myself if you'd been hurt." Coppersmith dragged his gaze away from the student and focused entirely on his own lover. It was as if the pair were alone, as if there wasn't a madman standing three yards from them, as if nobody existed in the whole world but themselves. Except that Stewart's gaze never wavered from the younger man.

"Idiot. It wouldn't have been your fault and that you

Lessons in Love

know very well. But it's over, Orlando, not just this afternoon but this whole wretched business. Over and done at last and I'm so glad." Jonty contemplated the lad who had minutes ago been threatening his very life and felt nothing but pity. He could feel no anger or fear now, just a desperate sadness that this young life was soon to be heading for the noose or more likely incarceration in an asylum, wasted and spent before it had even had time to find itself.

Trumper in his turn stared at Coppersmith and Stewart. Jonty could not credit the change in the lad's expression, bewilderment replacing certainty, fear replacing determination. He wondered whether Trumper had any comprehension that there could be tenderness between two men, rather than brutality and domination. It was like Coppersmith and the ideas he'd got from those wretched books, before Jonty had shown him that true love was kind and tender. "It's done with now, Mr. Trumper. Come, let's go and see Dr. Peters."

"No, Dr, Stewart, I don't think I'm ready for that. I know what I have to do." He darted down, picked up the razor before the other men could stop him and stood by the fireplace, seemingly transfixed by the tableau before him. He no longer appeared terrifying, just perplexed and sad. He heard the heavy footsteps on the stairs before either Stewart or Coppersmith did and he swung to face the door, mouth open.

Inspector Wilson burst into the room just in time to hear Trumper say, "I'm so sorry for the mess this is going cause, Dr. Stewart," before the lad raised the razor and quite unemotionally cut his own throat.

Dr. Peters insisted that Coppersmith and Stewart spend at least the Sunday night in sick-bay. He was backed up by the college nurse, who countered all their arguments and assertions that they would be fine with a tone more suited to addressing six year old boys with the measles. They would not be fine, they were coming to sick bay, she'd find them some pajamas herself and she'd be administering hot water bottles, cocoa and a sedative in that order. They both struck their colors in the face of this broadside and in the end they were mightily relieved they had.

Hot water bottles, cocoa and biscuits produced a comforting atmosphere, reminiscent of the nursery, and while they remained deeply disturbed about the afternoon's events, so disturbed that they could not even discuss them with each other, they found enough relaxation to fall asleep, aided by the largest dose of sedative that Mrs. Hatfield, the nurse, had dared give.

When midnight struck, the air was rent by screams as Stewart woke gasping for breath from a nightmare full of razors and ridiculously polite madmen who smiled and apologized as they killed. Mrs. Hatfield arrived, starched apron pulled hastily on over her nightgown, to find Coppersmith gently cradling his friend and crooning to him.

"Let me attend to him, Dr. Coppersmith, you need your sleep, too."

"No, ma'am. Dr. Stewart is my best friend, I was the one there with him when it happened and it's my duty to look after him now."

"But, Dr Cop..."

"You will but me no buts, thank you very much, Mrs. Hatfield." He fixed the lady with a very stony eye. "I'd be extremely obliged if you could make us another cup of cocoa, but I have the situation here under control." He laid Jonty's head gently against his own breast; the nurse saw that all argument was useless and scuttled off to the kitchen.

"It was awful, Orlando." Stewart spoke at last, once the cocoa had come, their jailer had departed again and they were confident she wouldn't return until morning. "I don't think I'll ever get the picture out of my head."

Coppersmith smoothed the hair from his friend's face. "Do you know, for the first time in my life I have someone to look after, someone who relies on me. I can't believe I've been so blessed." He kissed Jonty's cheek. "You will lose that picture, Jonty, believe me. Time is the best healer, you should know that."

"I do know it in my brain, but my heart's struggling with it at the moment." Jonty looked up into the chocolate brown eyes that were the sum of his content this night; there was no other comfort he could feel but the love of this dear, dear man. For all that the last few hours had been horrible for them both, it was wonderful to be in his lover's arms once more. "You've amazed me again, Orlando. You seem so strong, so much more able to cope than I've been."

Coppersmith seemed to require an eternity of thought before he replied. "I've seen a man slash his throat before, Jonty. I eventually got over the shock, although my mother never did." Tears began to well in his eyes. "I was only fourteen and, as you've no doubt guessed, the man was my father."

Jonty gasped, totally lost for words. He tentatively reached for his friend's hand. "I had no idea, honestly. Not the first notion."

"I've never spoken of it to anyone. I didn't speak at all for a month after it happened and had nightmares for two years afterwards."

And cut yourself off from the world for another decade, Jonty reflected, although he didn't dare say it. Another part of the puzzle that was Orlando Coppersmith began to slot into the overall picture. "Would you have ever told me, if this hadn't happened?"

"I would like to think so. At some point, I would have tried to." Now the tears flowed in rivers down Orlando's cheeks and Jonty mopped them with his eiderdown, risking the wrath of the nurse and not caring a hoot.

"Well you've astounded me yet again, Orlando. If it had been me endured all that, I would have gone to pieces in that room today. You're so brave. So very brave." He pulled Coppersmith's face towards him and kissed his brow. It tasted of sweat and something that wasn't normally there.

Jonty wondered if it were fear.

"It's different now. I'm not a boy anymore, and I have someone who loves me and needs me." He stroked Stewart's face in return. "I wish my fingers could speak for me. I can move you much more easily with touch than with words." Orlando sighed, shivered. "You do love me, don't you? And you need me?"

"I've told you the first often enough and the second I feel now more than ever before. Will you look after me?"

"I'll never stop, Jonty." Coppersmith placed another kiss on his friend's cheek—if the nurse came in, she'd have to lump it. "You'll get over this, much quicker than I did. You're a stronger person inside than I ever was."

"Don't know about that, Orlando. Don't think you ever really get over these things. You recover, yes, get on with your life, but it's not the same life as before."

"Indeed it isn't, Jonty." They snuggled down in the same bed, Orlando lying just under the eiderdown for propriety's sake, although they couldn't have cared less at that moment if Mrs. Hatfield had come in and found them *in flagrante delicto*. It was comfort they both needed, not the illusion of respectability.

And when the nurse brought them their tea and biscuits in the morning she did indeed find them still in the same bed, lying with arms entwined and faces peaceful. *Just like two little boys with the measles*, she thought kindly, being an innocent soul and having no real idea why any of the St. Bride's murders could have happened, the victims being *such nice young men*.

Two days later, Stewart returned to his rooms. Coppersmith had offered to swap sets with him, but Jonty had graciously declined. "I'd still have to go back to that room at some point, Orlando, and sooner is better than later. Can't carry on living in fear, you know." His wan smile had been growing brighter this last day, although the true

Lessons in Love

brilliance of Stewart's grin would take a while to be achieved.

The rooms had been cleaned from ceiling to floor, Miss Peters, the Master's sister, leading a band of bedders with strong stomachs in the unpleasant task. There were flowers in the room and most of Stewart's disorder had been replaced much as it had been before the place had seen violation. The rug had been replaced with a beautiful new red one, although Coppersmith couldn't help thinking fondly of the old blue one on which he and Jonty had frolicked the afternoon he got tipsy. His thoughts grew less fond when he considered what that carpet must be looking like at this exact moment.

"Will it do?" Orlando was reluctant to say anything more.

"Aye, it will. Once I've got my own clutter back how I like it." Stewart turned and kissed his friend on the cheek in a gesture speaking of dismissal. Maybe it wasn't yet time for the two of them to be alone here together. "I'll see you at hall tonight."

Coppersmith must have recognized that he was being sent away and complied, looking puzzled and concerned.

They met at hall and sat in their own chairs afterwards but life had changed, just as Jonty had predicted. His easy banter had disappeared and the spark of erotic tension that usually fizzed between them had been dampened. They spoke of mundane things—college business, university affairs—both afraid to touch on things that would be too painful, too frightening.

For a fortnight it remained so, the two men hardly touching either emotionally or physically, even on the night when Stewart had confessed that he was *sick and tired of having these wretched dreams and waking to an empty bed, so please may I share with you tonight, Orlando?* Share a bed they had, but no more than a kiss and caress otherwise.

Late February came and the two friends ventured for a walk along the Backs, by the river, admiring the first of the daffodils that were tentatively enjoying a lovely early spring day. They found the bench in the Fellows' Garden and sat, further apart now than they would have been had this walk been taken three weeks earlier.

"The crocuses are almost all done with, Dr. Coppersmith, and I don't think I noticed them at all this year."

"Quite understandable, we had other things on our minds." Orlando very tentatively reached a hand over and just grazed the side of Stewart's fingers, as he had the first night they'd been alone in his rooms, over the book of photographs.

Jonty sighed a deep sigh and very nearly smiled. "I didn't have one of those dreams last night. First time for a fortnight." He moved his hand closer to his friend's. "Woke up almost happy."

Orlando reached down, picked one of the last crocuses from among the grass and placed it in Stewart's palm. "Shall I tell you when I felt happy again? When I first knew real joy after my father's death?"

Jonty simply nodded, gently fingering the little purple bloom.

Coppersmith watched him intently, welcoming the small connection the flower made between them. "Here in this garden, after sliding half way along the Backs on that bloody ice. When you kissed me, I realized that I was healed at last." Orlando felt himself blush like the most simpering maiden from Girton and had to bow his head.

"You are such a big soft jessy, Dr. Coppersmith, and I love you more than I could possibly find words to say." Stewart laughed, as he hadn't laughed in weeks, until great drops rolled down his cheeks and turned into tears of sadness, released at last from the dam that had pent them since Trumper first took hold of the razor.

Orlando cried, too, as he had never cried in front of his

father or mother, having always been told that weeping was a sign of weakness and realizing now, at last, that it was just another aspect of strength and that crying with Jonty would always be acceptable. And his tears were both of sadness and joy, although whether he was happy that Jonty had at last said again that he loved him or whether it was because he had also called him *a big soft jessy* and was obviously coming back to his usual self, who could tell?

When the shedding of tears ended in the inevitable gulps for air, with eyes smarting against the light and horribly red rimmed, Jonty reached for Orlando's hand and pressed it. "We're very lucky to have each other. That poor lad Trumper, all he'd known was brutishness at the hands of another man, like those boys in the books that scared you so much. I've been wondering for so long why he cut his throat and I think I have it. I think we scared him; he saw us willingly offering to sacrifice ourselves and he couldn't understand what was going on. It didn't make any sense compared to what he'd experienced."

"And that was enough to make him kill himself?"

"I think he could live with certainty. He was sure he had a mission to kill men who lay with men and was happy to go through with it as his victims were fully deserving. When doubt came along, when he saw how much we meant to one another..." Jonty's voice faltered slightly and he seemed to be struggling for words.

"He couldn't live with doubts? With thinking he might just have been wrong about the others?" Orlando drew Jonty's hand to his mouth, kissed it gently.

"That's exactly it." Stewart suddenly stretched his arms and legs, like a cat in the spring sunshine. "I feel so much better, you know. I've spent so long worrying it was something I did or said that made that poor lad use the razor. But it wasn't, I'm sure of that now."

"I'm glad." Orlando gently rubbed the hand he held. "So what now? What's the next step in your recovery?"

"Bed, Dr. Coppersmith. Both of us, now? Well, don't

look so shocked, or did I forget to say please?" Jonty's grin shone more brightly than the February sun and in Orlando's humble opinion, it lit up the entire garden, the entire college, the entire world.

He grinned too. "Beautiful, magnificent, insatiable idiot are the words to be used, I seem to remember, Dr. Stewart."

"Shut up, Dr. Coppersmith and take me to that bed right now. I want to be healed, and your love's the best medicine."

The End

Turn the page for a look at

LESSONS IN DESIRE
Book Two:
A Cambridge Fellows Mystery

CHARLIE COCHRANE

Coming in February 2009
Brought to you by Linden Bay Romance

Chapter One

"A holiday will do us both the world of good." Jonty Stewart was sitting in his chair in the Senior Common Room of St. Bride's college, Cambridge, discussing the long vacation and plans he had for it. These, naturally, involved Orlando Coppersmith, who had usually holidayed by visiting other seats of learning, with the occasional dutiful visit to his grandmother in Kent interspersed among the academic outings. Orlando had no concept of just going off to some place of leisure and relaxing, frittering the time away on walks or sightseeing or bathing. His eyes grew wider as Jonty recounted the sort of things that *he'd* got up to in the past; the Riviera, visiting archaeological sites, cruising in the Mediterranean. This seemed to be yet another alien world that the sophisticated Stewart was introducing to his naïve friend. When Jonty suggested that they should go somewhere *together*, Orlando was appalled.

"Consider it, Dr. Coppersmith; the world is our oyster. Now, before you begin to quibble about the costs, I would remind you that my grandmother left her favorite grandson extremely well off, so money is no object. Name where you would like to go and we'll organize it. Shall it be Monte

Carlo or the rose red city of Petra?" A glorious smile lit Jonty's face as he made the suggestion.

"Must we go anywhere, Dr. Stewart?" Orlando was quite content here in his own college among the places and things that he knew well. No further unrest had come to St. Bride's since the murders of the previous winter, allowing his love affair with Jonty to blossom as beautifully as the magnolia trees which graced the Fellows' Garden. In his eyes, life was perfect here and now, so why should he go off searching for anything else?

Stewart looked mortally offended. "Of course we must. I have no intention of spending my long vac festering here. If you won't go with me, I'll go alone." He sniffed slightly. "Though I have gone alone on holiday too often in the past. I was hoping so very much that you would see fit to coming with me, so we could share the excitement. Think of the novelty, the exotic food, the flora and fauna that East Anglia can only dream of. Strange languages. Mysterious sights."

It was the novelty that Coppersmith couldn't stop thinking of, or so he told his friend. He'd encountered quite a lot of new things these last few months, particularly when he and Stewart were first acquainted. Now he was hoping for a period of relative calm before the new academic year ensued. The minute he looked into Jonty's eyes, he knew that he was beaten—the man desired this break so very much, the chance of a trip with his lover at his side. Who was Orlando to deny him it?

A compromise on the holiday was eventually reached. They would take a fortnight's leave, traveling no further than the Channel Islands; Stewart would find them some nice establishment on Jersey and book tickets for the ferry from Southampton. It would be adventurous, although not too much so, the food would be English (with perhaps a little native cuisine included) and there would be no language barrier. Orlando was particularly pleased about that, as modern languages were not his forte. Moreover, as he freely admitted, the thought of being around exotic foreign ladies terrified him.

For the next week Jonty beavered away with the Red Guide, simultaneously picking his mother's brains about hotels, the Honorable Mrs. Stewart being a great source of information about many things, until finally settling for The Beaulieu at St. Aubin's. "It boasts *three acres of terraced gardens with lawns, Private Tennis Courts, Fishing, and Bathing from the Hotel,*" he gleefully explained to his friend, waving the brochure about. "There are private bathrooms, so you won't risk ladies walking in on you should you forget to shoot the bolt. The additional cost for that will only be sixpence per night, so you won't be risking bankrupting me. Convenient for the train, too."

"It sounds delightful, Jonty," Coppersmith said, with *liar* written plain on his face. "You should book it."

"Already done, Orlando. They alleged that they were fully booked, August being high season, until they found themselves up against mama. She spoke to the manager, the owners, probably to King Edward himself; she's wangled us the best two-bedroomed suite in the house. I never really appreciated how wonderful it is to have quite such a formidable mother until now…"

"Do you still want *Jerusalem* at your funeral, Dr. Coppersmith?" Jonty began to gently rub his friend's back as the poor man clung to the ship's rail, green to the gills and desperately trying to fathom out whether he would feel better if he were sick again or not.

"I no longer care, Dr. Stewart. I think that I would prefer to die with the minimum of fuss, plus the maximum of expediency. I have enjoyed these last nine months, though I'm greatly afraid that I won't survive the journey." Orlando finished his speech with dignity, then sped off to the toilet to vomit again.

Jonty smiled sympathetically. He now felt a bit guilty about bringing his friend on this trip, but how was he to have any idea that Coppersmith would suffer quite so much from sea-sickness? Orlando hadn't even known it himself, having been on nothing more adventurous than the paddle steamer out of Ramsgate. There were at least two hours of the voyage left before they could feel decent, solid ground under their feet again. Then there was the awful prospect of having to do the journey all over again, back to Southampton, in a fortnight's time.

The nightmare of the crossing eventually ended, all the passengers reaching terra firma with much thanks. Coppersmith felt tempted to kneel down and kiss the very solid earth beneath his feet at the quay. Plenty of carriages were waiting for custom, so they were soon riding around the wide bay to St. Aubin's, able at last to admire the innocuous looking waters which had managed to wreak such havoc on a delicate digestive tract.

Orlando felt recovered enough to smile when he saw their hotel. It was everything that the rather overblown brochure had promised and more besides. Their bags were whisked away with just the right amount of efficient deference, the reception clerk was welcoming without being unctuous. Even the suite, once Coppersmith was entirely convinced that it was quite normal for friends of the same sex to take sets of rooms together, was pronounced to be above reproach.

They hadn't long begun to unpack before Stewart suggested that it was time to find a small sherry or some such before dinner. He assured his friend it would be entirely the right medicine to enable Coppersmith to recover his appetite so that he could tackle at least some of the delights that they'd spied on the hotel menu. Orlando felt rather affronted, wanting everything to have found its proper place before they ventured out, but Jonty insisted, so colors were struck. Coppersmith changed into his dinner jacket, newly purchased on Stewart's orders, as the old one looked more suited to the stalls at the music hall. Properly attired, they went down to the bar.

Lessons in Desire

The dining room was full, mainly married couples of various ages, from the bashful newlyweds who sat in the corner blushing at every remark that was made to them, to the elderly couple—all wrinkles and bright smiles—who sat at a table directly opposite the two Cambridge fellows. They had taken a great shine to the two young men as they'd chatted with them over pre-dinner drinks, insisting that they reminded them of their sons at a similar age. They seemed greatly impressed with Stewart's smile, his obvious good breeding and Coppersmith's beautiful manners. They made up a four for bridge in the sun lounge after dinner, proving excellent company, the lady in particular having an impish sense of humor. She chatted away to Jonty, the pair of them giggling like two schoolboys, despite her being old enough, just, to be his grandmother.

There were some families at dinner; two had brought their grown up daughters with them. Both girls were exceedingly plain and seemed rather smitten with the two young men, if blushes or girlish sighs were anything to go by. The only other unmarried couple present was a man perhaps three or four years older than Stewart, accompanied by what could only have been his father, given the strong family resemblance. The younger was a handsome chap whose dark curly hair framed deep blue eyes. Not that the two fellows of St. Bride's had eyes for anyone else, but one couldn't help noticing these things. They also couldn't help noticing the palpable tension that existed between the two men, shown in the strained politeness they showed to each other, the inability to keep eye contact between them. They had formed their own bridge four with another married couple, although they were obviously not having half the enjoyment that Coppersmith and his friend were.

Jonty was fascinated. He kept a surreptitious eye on them all evening, then bent Orlando's ear, back in their suite, over what might be going on.

"That young man's not happy to be here, Orlando. I think his father has made him come, while he'd rather be at home with his sweetheart, not entertaining a surly old curmudgeon." He turned to face the surly young curmudgeon who was struggling to arrange, into some sort of acceptable order, the mass of items that Stewart had strewn everywhere in an attempt to unpack.

"Nothing to do with us, Jonty." Coppersmith picked up the tie he'd worn for the journey, finding somewhere to put it carefully away.

"Aren't you even a little bit curious? This is such an opportunity of meeting new people, the sort of folk we might never meet at college. Like that delightful old couple; she certainly had the measure even of you at cards, Dr. Coppersmith." Stewart yawned, stretching like a great ginger cat. "This is going to be such a delightful holiday. The hotel is perfect, the food is excellent, I have great hopes for the company and you look less green than you did this morning. Such a lovely color in your cheeks now." He drew his hand down his lover's face, across his lips. It was the first time they'd touched with any degree of intimacy since they'd left St. Bride's. The caress made Orlando shudder afresh, as if they were touching for the first time. "We may have two bedrooms, Dr. Coppersmith, but do we really need to use them both? It'd be easy enough to slip across before the early morning tea arrives, if we set your alarm clock."

Orlando looked up, determined to refuse. He was still feeling exceedingly skittish about staying in a suite of rooms with his lover. Sharing a bed was beyond any imagining although, ironically, the item in question was a glorious double bed such as he'd dreamed, on many an occasion, of sleeping with Stewart in. "I'm not sure that I feel sufficiently recovered from the journey to want to do anything *except* sleep, Jonty." He studied his hands, awkwardly.

"That would be fine, Orlando. I'm as happy to simply slumber next to you as anything else. There are plenty of other days for romance; we could just be fond friends tonight, or pretend to be that old couple we played cards

Lessons in Desire

with. Still very much in love yet beyond the thralls of passion." Jonty gently touched his friend's hand.

Coppersmith felt as if a spider were crawling down the back of his neck, and his discomfiture must have been plain. "What if we slept apart, just for tonight?" They had reached the crux of why Orlando had been so keen not to come on holiday. He was frightened of taking their relationship outside the college walls, displaying it to the world. Within the ivy clad, male dominated locality of St. Bride's, it had been easy to maintain a friendship which was more than close without raising a suspicious eyebrow. He'd spent very little time with Jonty out of Cambridge, apart from a visit or two to London, where they'd stayed in the relatively safe environs of the Stewart family home. To be with the man in a strange place was to put himself at risk of making a demonstration of his affection by an unguarded look or touch. Any footman could walk through the streets of town in his bowler hatted Sunday best, hand in hand with a parlor maid. A pair of dons could never be allowed such freedom. Not in Cambridge and certainly not on Jersey.

Stewart slammed down the toothbrush he'd been unpacking. "Oh, you can go to sleep in the bath if you want to! I haven't the heart to put up with this nonsense. I'm going to sleep in my own bed, in my own soft pajamas, with my own book. If you change your mind and decide to join me, make sure you knock, because I might just have found other company." He spun on his heels, entering his bedroom with a slam of the door that caused the windows to shake.

Orlando contemplated opening the door again to give his friend a piece of his mind, but didn't want to end up in a full blown row in a public building. He also contemplated going in and giving Stewart the most comprehensive kissing he'd ever received. That was decided against, as it was probably exactly what the little swine wanted, so must be avoided at all costs. Even at the cost of a miserable night alone. Eventually, after tidying everything to his own immaculate standards, he trudged his weary way into his bedroom and readied himself for sleep.

At two o'clock in the morning, the heavens opened, torrential rain driving against the window panes while thunder pealed as loud as cannon fire. Orlando leapt out of bed without a second thought, making his way through their little sitting room into Jonty's bedroom. He didn't knock, knowing by now that any threats from Stewart about *finding company* were all bluster, to find his friend standing by the window, shivering.

"Come on, Jonty; you'll get cold, you know." Coppersmith put his arms around the man's shoulders, which felt icy through his silken pajama jacket. Stewart both hated thunderstorms and was fascinated by them. Orlando had often found him looking out of the window of his room at St. Bride's while the lightning rent the sky, making the college's very foundations seem to shake. Jonty could go into almost a dreamlike state, distracted and seemingly unaware of his surroundings, having to be coaxed back gently into the real world. Coppersmith did wonder whether some of the awful things which had happened to the man at school had taken place during storms, although he'd never been brave enough to ask.

Orlando gently took his lover to bed, tenderly soothing him back to sleep, holding tight as each new clap of thunder brought a shuddering through Jonty's frame. Eventually the storm passed eastwards and they could both fall asleep, Stewart as content as a child in his mother's arms. Coppersmith felt masterful, protective and very much in love. If anyone walked in, he had a legitimate medical excuse to be present. Or so he assured himself.

Thanks to Orlando's innate body clock, the chambermaid delivering the early morning tea found the two men in their own, separate beds, above reproach. Jonty soon brought his cup into Coppersmith's room and snuggled under the sheet, the night having been too muggy to occasion blankets. "Will you wear that tie today, Orlando, the one I bought you at Easter? The ladies would be very impressed."

Only a snort came in reply. "Most of the ladies I meet seem impressed at anything."

"Do you meet very many ladies, Orlando? Seems you're living a double life, then, because I never see you talking to them."

Coppersmith smote Stewart around the back of the head with his pillow. "Imbecile. Well, I'm going to take advantage of the *private bathroom at sixpence a night extra* to prepare myself for the day. You can shave at the basin while I'm in the tub."

Tea shot out of Jonty's nose, making him splutter in an undignified manner. The thought of Orlando issuing an invitation to be viewed in the bath—such a thing hadn't happened since the afternoon the man had got drunk at St. Thomas' college, not even when they'd shared a bathroom while staying at Stewart's family home. It seemed marvelously out of character. "I'll certainly take up the offer or we'll never see breakfast. I can smell the bacon already, although that might just be an olfactory illusion. Breakfast, then church, I saw you wince, but we *are* going, then off to the beach." Jonty squeezed his lover's thigh. "I saw you wince when I mentioned *beach* as well, so you'll just have to apply your stiff upper lip."

Jonty sat down on a rock to get on with removing his shoes and socks.

"What are you doing?"

"Going paddling, Orlando." The holiday air had affected them both, so using Christian names now seemed acceptable, even outside their suite. Stewart suddenly looked up at the awkward figure which towered over him. "Oh, Orlando. You'd never been in The Bishop's Cope, you'd never been punting, please, *please* don't tell me that you have never paddled."

"I have actually paddled on a number of occasions, when I was taken to see my grandmother at Margate." Orlando attempted to look a man at once dignified and completely au fait with the delights of the seaside.

Jonty assumed a particularly sly look. "When exactly was the last time you indulged in this wild activity?"

Coppersmith mumbled, "When I was seven."

Jonty giggled. "Then you had better ruddy well get your socks off and your trouser bottoms rolled up, because you are coming with me."

Orlando felt distinctly miffed. He contemplated refusing to do any such thing, but decided to obey orders, stuffing his socks into the toes of his shoes, then tying the laces together in imitation of Stewart. The reason for this strange procedure became obvious when Jonty slung his shoes around his neck, leaving his hands free to continue to pick up stones for skimming or shells for stuffing in his pockets.

As he watched Jonty turning over rocks to search for tiny crustaceans which he then let run over his palms, it struck Orlando more than ever that at heart his friend was just an overgrown boy. An enormous crab was rooted out, a good three inches across the carapace, which Stewart expertly picked up to wave at Coppersmith. "What a whopper, Orlando! Look!" He passed the creature over, grinning as his friend inevitably grabbed it the wrong way, earning a sharp nip on his fingers.

Coppersmith flung the offending animal away, shaking his sore hand and cursing like a sailor.

"Orlando, such language!" Jonty hooted with laughter. "Look, take him *across* the back, so all your fingers are out of his reach." He demonstrated the technique, then made his friend do the same.

Gingerly Orlando took up the vicious creature, breaking into a smile of delight when the method worked. "He's a beauty, Jonty. Not big enough for tea, though." Laughing, he placed the crab down among the rocks, returning to follow his friend. The tide was ebbing, revealing rock pools full of shrimps which Stewart caught in his hand, then let spring out of his grasp with a giggle. Coppersmith soon learned that game too, proving much more adept at catching the little invertebrates and the darting fishes than his friend. It was like being a child again, except that there hadn't been that much room for play in his childhood, so there was time to be caught up. Yet again, he could experience a freedom with Stewart that he'd never known before they met. He watched his friend pick up a huge ormer shell, holding it to the light so that they could both admire the mother of pearl glittering in the sunlight.

"Beautiful. Eh, Orlando?"

"Indeed." Although Coppersmith didn't mean the shell so much as the man holding it.

Tired, eventually, of annoying the occupants of the rock pools, they began to walk along the waterline, the warm sea just lapping over their feet. The occasional wave came in with slightly more force, making them jump out of the way, splashing and laughing.

It took a whole mile of wandering for Stewart to begin to make mischief, beginning to splash just a little too deliberately in a particular direction. Coppersmith didn't notice at first, blaming the splatters on his trousers purely on the swell. When he did realize exactly what was going on, he handled the situation admirably, deciding that revenge is a dish best eaten cold. While he would have loved to dunk Stewart completely, there and then, more pleasure was to be had by quietly removing himself from flying water range before making his plans.

Seaweed isn't the most pleasant thing to handle straight from the sea. It was disagreeable on the feet when it slipped around them in the water and it was truly disgusting when forcibly stuffed down the back of one's trousers. Jonty Stewart was made to suffer the worst of this punishment as Orlando executed his vengeance.

"You swine!"

"You're no longer dealing with some naïve young man who's spent all his days in a haze of academia. I'm learning, Dr. Stewart, so you'd better watch your step." Orlando looked wonderfully smug, strikingly handsome in his triumph.

Jonty fished down his pants to extract the offending piece of algae. He flung it at his friend, missed by a mile, then laughed. "I've only ever wanted you to be my equal, Orlando. I'm looking forward enormously to the day when you tease me both mercilessly and with aplomb." He reached out his hand to take Orlando's, must have remembered that they were in public, shrugged in apology and walked on.

They strolled the length of the beach, till Stewart's pockets were so full of shells that he'd begun to rattle. Drying off their feet on their handkerchiefs proved largely ineffective, as did hopping madly about so that the clean, dry foot couldn't be infected with sand before it made its way into its sock. Sand always found its way into every available crevice and was bound to begin to creep into their shoes regardless before they were halfway off the beach. The long walk back to Corbiere station would be uncomfortable, although it wouldn't spoil the delights of the previous hours.

Jonty felt the glow which always came with having enlightened his Dr. Coppersmith, introducing some new pleasure—innocent or not—into the man's life. Orlando had shown a spark of delight in having effectively taken a rare revenge on his friend. Stewart wondered whether he was plotting other ways of getting one over on him. *This holiday is showing every sign of being more than enjoyable.*

They saw the young man from the hotel on the station platform, looking much happier without his usual companion. He acknowledged them with a tilt of the head, which was all the encouragement that Stewart needed to effect an introduction. "I believe that you're staying at The Beaulieu as we are? My name is Stewart. This is my friend Coppersmith." Jonty waved his hand to indicate Orlando, who had yet to venture any closer.

"Ainslie is my name, sir. Matthew Ainslie. I'm delighted to meet you." The man held out his hand, producing a most engaging smile in the process.

"Have you been on Jersey long, Mr. Ainslie?"

"Matthew, I insist that you call me Matthew." He smiled again. "I...*we* arrived five days ago. My father and I always come to one of the Channel Islands once a year; he feels that the air agrees with him."

"Well, I hope that it will agree with us. It's our first time here and I've been very pleasantly surprised so far. I dare say that we'll be picking your brains about the best places to visit."

"Your friend over there is enjoying himself, too?" Ainslie indicated Orlando, who looked nothing like a man enjoying himself. A man trying to win the most surly face competition, perhaps.

"I believe he is, although he doesn't often show it. He enjoyed playing bridge last night with the Tattersalls. Such a delightful couple."

Ainslie smiled. "They beat us soundly on Friday night. I wouldn't like to meet Mrs. Tattersall in a rubber if high stakes were in order, although she could charm the birds out of the trees." His face suddenly changed. "Please excuse me. I can see my father—he'll want me to attend him." A smile and the man was gone, leaving Stewart's interest more piqued than ever.

After another excellent dinner, the fours for bridge were different from Saturday evening. The Ainslies played against Mrs. Tattersall, who was paired with Coppersmith, Jonty and Mr. Tattersall having opted to observe the fun. Orlando and partner trounced the opposition, even when they were obviously not trying, which made it ten times worse. The elder Ainslie's temper was beginning to fray as rubber after rubber went down, until he snapped at his son, on whom no blame could be fairly laid. Matthew was a far more competent player than his father.

For Jonty the fascination lay not with the play (that was a foregone conclusion) but in what the eyes around the table were doing. Coppersmith watched Ainslie's hands in fascination as he skidded the cards over the table. This man was a talented shuffler and dealer, the sort who would be interesting to see playing alongside a competent partner. While Coppersmith watched Matthew's hands, the man watched his. Orlando had long, delicate fingers, fingers with which Jonty was intimately acquainted, which he found beautiful. Ainslie followed the graceful movements Coppersmith's digits made as they picked up and sorted his hand, caressing the backs of the cards.

Jonty observed the way that Ainslie was watching. He would not forget it.

About the Author:

Charlie Cochrane's ideal day would be a morning walking along a beach, an afternoon spent watching rugby, and a church service in the evening, with her husband and daughters tagging along, naturally. She loves reading, theatre, good food, and watching sport.

She started writing relatively late in life but draws on all the experiences she's hoarded up to try to give a depth and richness to her stories.

Also by Charlie Cochrane:

Aftermath in Trilogy No. 111: Speak Its Name

Expectations riding on a generation of young Englishmen are immense; for those who've something to hide, those expectations could prove overwhelming.

When shy Edward Easterby first sees the popular Hugo Lamont, he's both envious of the man's social skills and ashamed of finding him so attractive. But two awful secrets weigh Lamont down. One is that he fancies Easterby, at a time when the expression of such desires is strictly illegal. The second is that an earlier, disastrous encounter with a young gigolo has left him unwilling to enter into a relationship with anyone. Hugo feels torn apart by the conflict between what he wants and what he feels is "right". Will Edward find that time and patience are enough to change Hugo's mind?

This is a publication of
Linden Bay Romance
WWW.LINDENBAYROMANCE.COM

Recommended Read:

Captain's Surrender by Alex Beecroft

Ambitious and handsome, Joshua Andrews had always valued his life too much to take unnecessary risks. Then he laid eyes on the elegant picture of perfection that is Peter Kenyon.

Soon to be promoted to captain, Peter Kenyon is the darling of the Bermuda garrison. With a string of successes behind him and a suitable bride lined up to share his future, Peter seems completely out of reach to Joshua.

But when the two men are thrown together to serve during a long voyage under a sadistic commander with a mutinous crew, they discover unexpected friendship. As the tension on board their vessel heats up, the closeness they feel for one another intensifies and both officers find themselves unable to reign in their passion.

Let yourself be transported back to a time when love between two men in the British Navy was punishable by death, and to a story about love, about honor, but most of all, about a *Captain's Surrender*.

Printed in the United States
209654BV00003B/12/P